The Retreat

The Retreat

A Tale of Spiritual Awakening

Jacci Turner

HARPER LEGEND

HARPER LEGEND

HarperCollins books may be purchased for educational, business, or sales promotional use. For information, please e-mail the Special Markets Department at SPsales@harpercollins.com.

FIRST HARPERCOLLINS PAPERBACK EDITION PUBLISHED IN 2018

Cover design © HarperCollins
Book design by SBI Book Arts, LLC

ISBN 978-0-06-267464-7

To Amy Hauptman—my sunshine friend.
Thank you for raising money for me to go to the
"grounding retreat," where this book was born.
You are amazing.

The Retreat

1

How did I end up at a Benedictine monastery in Nebraska? The question circled through Amy's mind as she walked gingerly around the man-made lake behind the monastery.

Truth was, she knew exactly how she'd gotten here. It was Jennie's fault. Jennie, her college roommate and the kindest person Amy knew, had not only insisted she come, she'd raised the money to pay for it. Jennie had been to the retreat a year before and said it changed her life.

Her mind went back to the day she'd come home from a class for her graduate degree in social work. Her mom always left her mail on the small table next to her bed. There was a card from Jennie, with a cryptic note, and a check for seventy-five dollars. The note said, "You need to come to this retreat with me. It will be amazing." That was all—that and a web address for the "Contemplative Activists" website.

Amy knew what activists were. Her father had called her and Jennie "firebrands" in college. They were leaders in their campus Christian club: organizing food drives, bringing in guest speakers on child soldiers, and more. Then, upon graduation, they'd both gone off to save the world. Amy had gone to Thailand to work with a group that rescued girls and women from sex trafficking, and Jennie to Chicago to help underserved kids.

Amy checked the Contemplative Activist website and got a vague sense of this supposedly special place in Nebraska.

As Amy walked in the dark, she passed other retreatants who smiled or nodded in the dim light. It felt good to move her body after a whole day of flying to get here. The air was soft on her face. Her skin felt like silk in this humidity. Being from Nevada, where the air was dry as toast, the moisture felt like a gift. The August air was warm and the light breeze caressed her.

She remembered texting Jennie back immediately after checking out the website. "Thank you so much! I can't believe you did that." Jennie worked for a nonprofit. She didn't have seventy-five dollars to give away. She'd continued her text: "But I can't possibly afford the retreat. I will rip up the check."

Jennie had fired back another cryptic remark. "Just wait a few weeks."

Amy took a fork in the path that led down to a tall statue of a monk. His arms stretched out over the pond, and floodlights shooting up made it look like he was celebrating after a touchdown. An illuminated nameplate at the base of the statue read, St. Benedict. She knew nothing of the saint but decided to call him Benny and that he must be a 49er. She loved the 49ers and had attended many games with her grandpa, her Opa who had lived near San Francisco and had been a die-hard fan.

She enjoyed being out in the dark without fear that someone would attack her. The other retreatants were nearby and it seemed like a safe place. There was a fountain in the lake behind her that made a peaceful sound as its gentle splashing mingled with the chirp of crickets and cicadas. Hadn't Tom, the retreat leader, said to be sure to look at the stars tonight? She walked back up the path and found one of the many benches that lined it. Lying back, she put her feet on the bench, knees bent, and stared up at the stars. Amy was impressed. In Reno you couldn't really see the stars unless you left town. The lights of the twenty-four-hour city drowned out the sky. There was only one word to describe this night: it was *thick* with stars. Thick. If she'd known anything about constellations, she probably could have found them all. As it was, she could only find the big and small dippers, an accomplishment she equated to playing "Chopsticks" on the piano. Jennie could have named them all, oh why wasn't she here?

True to Jennie's word, cards had begun arriving in the mail. They were from people Amy hadn't talked to in a long time, friends that had been in her Bible study during college. Freshmen that she and Jennie had taken under their wings. They were grown and gone now, with budding careers of their own. All included notes with their small checks, saying things like, "You made a difference in my life; I'm glad to give a little back." She'd been shocked. She felt so separated from those days. From that kind of faith. She felt like a hypocrite. Should she even take their money? What would they think of her now, their former Bible study leader, a failure as a missionary, a failure as a church leader, a failure as a Christian?

But suddenly she had the money, not only for the five-day retreat, but also for the trip there and back. Reluctantly she'd registered—if nothing else, she'd get a week with Jennie. She should be studying. She should be looking for work. She should be doing a lot of things, but the idea of getting to see Jennie after two years had been too tempting.

Then Jennie had dropped the bomb. Her folks had decided to fly to Chicago that weekend to surprise her with a visit. She couldn't come to the retreat and Amy had already registered and bought her plane tickets. She'd thought about backing out, but what about all those people who had sent money?

Now Amy was in Nebraska at a retreat center with fifty strangers from twenty different states. She gazed at the sky as a falling star streaked across her vision and went out. Wasn't she supposed to make a wish? *I wish I were anywhere but here.*

2

Amy woke up in a daze. It felt like the middle of the night. Why was her alarm going off? She reached over the side of the bed where her phone was charging on the floor and shut off the noise. It said seven o'clock in the morning.

She sat up on the bed, trying to focus her blurry eyes, totally disoriented. She was in a room with two twin beds, one of them empty. A crucifix hung across from her on the wall. The retreat center. The empty bed was where Jennie was supposed to sleep. The room was simple: a soft chair under the window that looked out on the grounds, a desk and chair under the crucifix, and a bathroom. She was so tired. It was five A.M. in Reno—why was she up?

Amy fumbled around the table next to her bed and flipped on the small lamp, blinking at the light. She grabbed the name tag she'd been given at registration, with its black lanyard and plastic rectangular pouch. The front declared Amy Spanier—Reno. She flipped it over and squinted at the back, where the conference's schedule had been printed. Seven thirty Monday was breakfast and eight thirty was yoga. Ah, breakfast—that's why she wanted to get up at "the butt crack of dawn," as her best friend, Joshua, would say. They were smart not to put yoga first on the schedule. She could have easily talked herself out of that, but breakfast? Amy was a girl who liked to eat. Not that she was fat, but she wasn't skinny either. Her Opa had described her as "sturdy," a description she rather enjoyed.

As she pulled on her workout clothes, she thought of the woman who had picked her up from the airport. She was a tiny, beautiful Muslim named Amani. Tom, the retreat leader, had arranged the ride and Amy was thankful not to have to rent a car after Jennie canceled on her. Amani had a large poster board in the car and Amy, pointing at the board, had said, "I can tell you're a teacher," to break the ice. She actually already knew that Amani was a teacher, because Tom had told her in an e-mail. Amani said, "Yes, but actually the poster is my 'thirty things to do before I turn thirty' board. I want to fill it out while I'm here."

That thought had captured Amy's attention immediately. She had turned twenty-nine just last month and decided right then to make her own list. If she got nothing else out of this week, she'd have a list of things to try before she turned thirty. That sounded fun.

Would she like yoga? If she did, it could be something to put on her list. She needed to do something physical. She'd definitely slacked on the exercise since—well, since Westin Timothy Davis, to be exact.

West was her almost fiancé, now ex–almost fiancé. Who was now the fiancé of someone else. That piece of . . . Amy grabbed her pillow and screamed into it until the frustration ebbed. She stood, panting, as thoughts of West floated into her mind, a scowl across his handsome face. "I don't think we're on the same page anymore, Amy," he had said. *Whatever.* She pushed him from her mind, throwing the pillow against the far wall.

She went to the sink to brush her teeth. The fluorescent light was not kind. She was confronted with a bush of wild brown curls where her once-tame hair had been. It was the humidity. It gave her "Hermione hair." That's what Joshua called this look, after her favorite Harry Potter character. Oh well—she was just going to yoga, right? It had been what—nine years since she'd tried yoga? She'd taken it for a P.E. credit in college her freshman year. *I hope I don't embarrass myself.*

She grabbed her brush and pulled a hair tie off the handle, tying the whole mane of hair back in a loose ponytail at the crown of her head. She checked the mirror. Wiping sleep from her blue eyes, she noticed dark circles. She was not going to worry about that right now; in fact, she just might go the whole week without makeup. She'd never see these people again anyway, right? She checked the mirror once more. Not great, but good enough. She needed coffee.

Snatching her travel mug from her suitcase, she walked down a carpeted hall to the other end of the building, passing other groggy retreatants. Some smiled, some nodded, and some kept their eyes down. They probably needed coffee too. The walls were lined with pictures of priests or biblical scenes. She'd never been in a Catholic retreat center before and it felt foreign, like being in a different country.

The hallway opened up into a bigger area. Their meeting room was on the right, and to the left was a large bank of windows that led outside to the path around the lake. She glanced out at the morning, the sky a slate gray. Following the direction the others were going, she found a small drink station next to the dining hall and filled her travel mug with coffee, adding two yellow sweetener packets and two little pots of French vanilla creamer. Joshua's voice rang through her head: "You like candy, not coffee."

He would know. As a barista at Starbucks, he always had a cup ready for her in the morning. But she did not look forward to the quip that came with it. She had a sweet tooth, it was true, and he loved to playfully tease her about it.

Only one cup, she promised herself. She'd overdone the caffeine on the three planes yesterday (that's what a cheapo ticket got you) and had found it hard to get to sleep. She sat her cup on one of the long, empty tables in the dining room. That would force her to meet people when all she wanted to do was crawl into a cave. She'd come all the way to godforsaken Nebraska—she had to figure out why, and she wasn't going to find out if she kept to herself the whole week. If God was going to speak to her—and Amy was not at all sure he would—he usually did so through other people, at least he had in the past.

She joined the line outside the food bar that led into a room where two stainless-steel tables were filled with breakfast options. She watched the people in front of her grab trays and silverware off the back wall unit, then go to either side of the buffet. She slid a tray off the stack and headed to the right side. The first station had fresh fruit, and she loaded her plate. *I'd better pace myself,* she thought. Five days of buffets would be a killer on her figure. She'd already packed on a few extra pounds, Post West or "PW," as Joshua had tagged her breakup with West, and it was time to start eating healthier. Maybe she'd put that on her "thirty before thirty" list. Lose ten pounds.

As the line progressed, she observed the other retreatants. Some were her parents' age, but most were around her age or a few years older. Some were in pairs, but most appeared to be alone. Most were white, but there were a few people of color.

She came to the next station: eggs, sausage, and bacon. She put a small amount of each on her plate and spooned salsa onto her eggs. She wondered about Amani. Would there be food here she could eat? She knew Muslims didn't eat pork. Maybe she should offer to make a food run for her. Of course, she'd have to borrow Amani's car. That was silly. She had a lot of thoughts like that, wanting to be helpful without realizing how impossible it was.

The next station was bread—better skip that. Her tray loaded, she went back to find her coffee cup. Two girls, about her age, were at the table facing her. "Mind if I join you?" she asked.

They both smiled at her in welcome. The one on her left had a short, asymmetrical brown bob, pore-less skin, and large Bambi eyes. "Please do. I'm Natalie," she said.

Amy slid into the chair, placing her tray on the table. "I'm Amy."

"Brooke," said the other girl, rounder, with her blond hair pulled back in a severe ponytail. Her dimples were epic. "We were just talking about documentaries. Do you like them?" Her voice was strong, confident.

"I do," said Amy. She watched an occasional documentary.

Natalie's eyes got even bigger. "I just love them. I just watched this one on whales; do you know that people didn't start to save the whales until they learned that whales could sing? That made them more human, and suddenly activists stepped in to keep them from being slaughtered." Natalie talked without taking a breath as if whales were the most important subject in the world.

Brooke chimed in. "I love the ones about sustainable fashion. Do you know that most of the clothes we buy are made in sweatshops by children?"

Amy was starting to get the gist of the conversation. The conference *was* for activists after all. Everyone here was probably concerned about justice issues. But these girls seemed so young. As her Opa would have said, they were "bright eyed and bushy tailed." Suddenly Amy felt like a wrung-out dishrag, too cynical and old beyond her years.

They prattled on happily about documentaries they'd watched on genetically modified food and puppy mills. Amy wondered when she'd become so cynical. When she said she liked documentaries, she'd meant a more frivolous variety. Like the one about the guy who spent a year living off whatever he could find on Craigslist. Suddenly the topic switched to TED Talks. Now that was something she could talk about.

"I love TED Talks," she volunteered.

"Me too," said Natalie, leaning forward as if TED Talks were the most important thing in her life. Amy wondered if she spoke about everything with perky enthusiasm. She had to push down a smile thinking of Natalie gushing about Pap smears or root canals. If only Joshua were here to laugh with her.

Natalie continued. "I just love Elizabeth Gilbert. *Eat, Pray, Love* was my favorite book. Some of my friends were like, 'Really? *Eat, Pray, Love*?' But yeah, *Eat, Pray, Love*!"

Amy knew what she meant. Since this was a largely Christian retreat, Natalie was probably from an evangelical Christian background like herself. That particular brand of Christian tended to look askance at anything that smacked of Eastern mysticism, and Elizabeth Gilbert's book had a whole section on the joys of meditation. Amy had loved it. She remembered when she'd been judgmental like that, though. In fact, in the not-too-distant past, riding to a Catholic retreat center with a Muslim would have felt really weird. When had she changed?

"Oh, I loved that book," agreed Brooke, "but the movie was eh," she said, moving her hand, palm down, back and forth to signal the movie was only so-so. "Have you watched the TED Talks by Brené Brown? I love her. I saw her live in Boston."

"Oh, I love her!" said Natalie. "I didn't know she did live presentations."

"Oh yeah," said Brooke. "Have you read *Rising Strong*? That book came at just the right time for me. I was hired at a church to be the youth pastor and it was a disaster."

Amy perked up at this. "Really? I just got fired from a church myself!"

"No way," said Brooke.

"That's amazing, guys," broke in Natalie. "I really want to hear about it, but it's time for yoga. Do you want to go?"

"I do," said Brooke. "We'll have to talk later, Amy. I can't wait to hear your story."

Amy grabbed her tray and followed the girls out. Was it possible that someone here could relate to her pain? Maybe she had more in common with these girls than she knew.

3

Yoga felt wonderful. The teacher was Felicia, the tiny blond wife of the man who had spoken last night, Tom. They were leading the retreat together and were both shorter than Amy's five foot ten. They were what Tom jokingly referred to as "fun sized."

"What is your intention for this practice?" asked Felicia to the thirty people on mats. *My intention is to survive,* thought Amy. Then she revised, *It's to stretch. I really feel tight.*

They were in the same room they'd started in last night but the large circle of chairs had been removed and now yoga mats filled the space in haphazard rows. Violin music played in the background as Felicia's comforting voice spoke to them. She led in a way that Amy instantly clicked with: "This is your practice," she said. "Listen to your body. If a move is not working for you, adjust until it is." Amy loved that and was able to do all the moves Felicia led them through even though she was nowhere as graceful as Natalie on the mat next to her.

After the workout, Amy had time to go back to her room to shower. She headed down the hall, promising to see her new friends at the next meeting. Last night's meeting had been more of an introduction. "This is your retreat," emphasized Tom. "If you need to skip a meeting, skip it. Make it whatever you need."

Amy liked that too. She wasn't used to Christian retreats with so much permission and space. They were usually filled to the brim with mandatory meetings and seminars with no time to breathe. And she also noticed that neither Tom nor Felicia used Christianese, the trite Christian language that most believers used and that she was sick to death of. It was refreshing to hear faith talked about in different terms, because the old terms were definitely not working for her anymore.

Last night, Felicia had oriented them to the facility: be on time for meals, keep your key on you at night because the doors lock at eight—that sort of thing. Then one of the German monks who lived at the monastery had come in to welcome them. Amy adored his accent; it reminded her of her Grandpa Franz, her Opa, who had come to America as a teenager. He'd died this January, right after the new year. Oma, her grandmother, said he'd just wanted to get through the holidays one more time. To Amy, his death was just one more crappy thing in her life, like the frosting on a dung cake. Amy smiled at that—a dung cake! She really needed to learn how to swear. A tear fell unbidden down Amy's cheek as she fumbled with the key to her room. The last five years had been rough, and she missed the gentle man who had guided her through it and called her his "precious Amy."

Inside Amy bent down to untie her shoe and was amazed that she had no trouble reaching her feet. *Wow,* she thought, *that stretch intention thing really worked!* She went to her bed, opened her notebook, pulled out a pen, and wrote, "Thirty things to do before I turn thirty," then added the first two: "One: lose ten pounds. Two: start taking yoga."

As she showered, she let her mind wander back to last night's session. She knew what activism was, but what exactly was contemplation? It sounded like navel-gazing to her, and wasn't that the polar opposite of activism?

Tom had explained that they were going to be learning and trying what he called "contemplative practices." He talked about how he and Felicia had worked for twenty years with marginalized populations overseas, boy soldiers, refugees, and trafficked girls and women. She'd have to talk to him about that. Compare notes.

He said that they'd noticed a high burnout rate for those in his organization and in other helping professions too, like social work and teaching. She could relate to that. Burned to a crispy critter—that was her. She felt like she'd been running a marathon for the last six years. All she really wanted to do was check out of the human race.

So he and Felicia had started interviewing leaders of the contemplative movement to see what they could do to keep the staff from crashing. They talked to Richard Rohr, Thomas Keating and Mother Teresa. The only name she'd recognized from that list was Mother Teresa, but if Tom and Felicia had gone and hung out with her, they were the real deal in Amy's mind. Anyway, Tom said they believed that contemplative practices were the missing ingredient. He said if you could marry activism and contemplative practices, it would sustain the difficult works.

Amy dried off and dressed. She wasn't sure she'd be trying any more "difficult works" in this lifetime. The last two she'd tried had failed miserably and she'd ended up without a job and living with her parents at twenty-eight years of age. After letting her lick her wounds for two months, her parents had asked her to sit down in the living room "for a little chat."

"We're worried about you, Amy," her mother had said. "It's time you got a job, or—have you considered graduate school?" Her mother was clearly uncomfortable having this conversation.

Her father took over. "Remember the rule," was all he had to say. That rule—"If you're going to live at home, you need to be working or going to school full time"—was basically made up for her younger brother Seth. He didn't know what to do with himself after high school and had chosen to join the army rather than take classes. Amy, the responsible one, had never thought that rule would apply to her.

Amy decided to go to graduate school and chose social work because it was the fastest master's she could get that made a person

employable. That and nursing, but Amy tended to be squeamish
at the sight of blood. She only had to take a few prerequisites and
a one-year program of study. She'd finished the class work and
was now ready for her thesis. The problem was, she had no idea
what she wanted to do it on, and the proposal was due next week.
Another reason she shouldn't have come here.

She tried to tame her hair, thinking about how last night had
ended. Tom had led them into the chapel. It was lit only by candles
on an altar that was surrounded on three sides by chairs. It was
dark inside and smelled of incense, but she could tell the ceilings
were high and the room was huge. She'd have to come back during
the day.

He'd led them through what he called an examen. It had five
parts, but Amy could only remember two. The first one was what
Tom called "looking for a consolation from the day." You were
supposed to sift through the day and look for a place you felt
at peace, a place you felt truly yourself, safe. A place where you
noticed the Divine touching your life.

That was hard for Amy. After three airplanes and the insecuri-
ties that had assailed her about coming here alone, how could she
find a consolation? The room was big and still; people sat spaced
apart and silent. Tom's quiet voice prompted them. "It is like rum-
maging in your bag for your keys," he said, "to find something
that you know was there but might have missed unless you really
looked."

Finally, Amy's brain snagged a moment. It was when Joshua
had dropped her off at the airport. He was her best, and pretty
much only, friend left in Reno. Only a true friend would get up at
four in the morning to take you to the airport. She'd have asked
her parents, but they were gone for the weekend and Joshua said
there was no way he was letting her take an Uber. When he got
out of the car and set her travel bag on the ground, he'd pulled her
into a tight hug. Joshua was shorter than her and stick thin, but for

one moment she felt safe. She didn't want to leave that embrace, but finally, Joshua pushed away from her and said, "You'll be fine, Pooh Bear! Go—and text me!" And she'd gone. But that one hug had felt good. Safe. She chose it as her consolation.

She looked at her reflection in the bathroom mirror. Maybe just a little concealer. You never know—there were a lot of good-looking guys here. She mentally kicked herself for even thinking of that, and applied the concealer anyway.

As Tom led them through the examen last night, he had also said they were supposed to look for a time of desolation: a place in the day where they'd missed the Divine, not been their true self, not been at peace. Amy's mind had swarmed with images then, too many to count. She finally landed on the little hissy fit she'd thrown after she'd found her room and she realized that there was no cell phone signal inside the monastery. Not only would she not have access to the Internet, but she wouldn't even be able to text. She'd been mad! Later she'd found that she could get a weak signal if she went outside, but how often would she have a chance to do that? She remembered her desolation, the temper tantrum. Even though no one saw it, she felt ashamed of herself. Was she really one of those people who couldn't survive without her phone?

Tom had ended the examen with the reminder that tomorrow was another day and that a new day would bring hope. Well, today was that new day, and it was time for their first session. She would see if it came with hope or not.

4

The chairs in the large meeting room were back in a huge circle. The white walls were bare and the overhead lights were bright. Last night, when they'd all introduced themselves, Amy had said, "I'm Amy, from Reno. My friend Jennie came here and loved it so much she actually raised money for me to come." The whole room had said, "Ahhhhh." Yep, Jennie got that reaction from people even when she wasn't there.

Now, Amy found a chair and was glad when Brooke and Natalie came in and sat on either side of her.

Felicia, the petite, pretty blonde who looked twenty but Amy guessed must be closer to forty if they'd been doing this work for twenty years, waited until the room was full and then told them to sit comfortably on their "sit bones," which Amy took to mean her tailbones. Felicia modeled quickly, pulling at her thighs. "You might need to *lift the gift* to find your sit bones." Amy laughed along with the others—she definitely had a gift to lift. She settled back into her chair and put her feet on the floor.

"Now," Felicia continued, "take some breaths from your diaphragm. Three diaphragm breaths will start to reset your parasympathetic nervous system." Amy closed her eyes and breathed deeply. It felt like she'd been starved for air and didn't even know it. Her abdomen swelled and she breathed in through her nose and out through her mouth. It felt good. When had she started breathing so shallowly?

Felicia continued. "We will be breathing through a scripture from the Hebrew Bible in declining increments. Just repeat after me and we'll end with the tone." She waited a moment and then began slowly. "Be still and know that I am God."

Amy repeated with the rest of the group, "Be still and know that I am God."

"Be still and know that I am," said Felicia.

"Be still and know that I am," said Amy.

"Be still and know."

"Be still and know."

"Be still."

"Be still."

"Be."

"Be."

Amy liked the way that sounded. She breathed deeply and then there was a sound, like a low gong that rang three times and vibrated for a few seconds after the last tone. She opened her eyes to see Felicia holding some kind of bronze bowl and wooden stick with its end wrapped in a red cloth.

"We hope you all slept well," said Tom. "We know it was really hard for all of you to come here, taking time away from your busy lives and good work. We honor your sacrifice." Tom had long, blond hair dusted with gray that he had tied back in a ponytail. His facial hair was cut like Abraham Lincoln's, a thin line around his jaw that ended in a generous chin beard. It was not a style Amy liked, but somehow it made Tom seem cool.

"Let me tell you about today," he continued. "This morning we will look at the history of the contemplative movement; then we do our first practice. After today's practice, you will be in your triad to debrief the exercise. A few groups will have four people. The names for your triad are on the back of your name tags." Amy lifted hers and was disappointed to see neither Brooke nor Natalie listed there.

"Just find somewhere, around the building or outside, to meet with your triad and introduce yourselves briefly. Spend as long as you need debriefing the practice. At twelve we have lunch. Then, for those that signed up, we will meet in here at one for a new practice, and debrief." Amy remembered that she had signed up for every single extra session. Hey, if she was coming all the way to Nebraska, she might as well wring the life out of the experience. "Then each day," Tom continued, "except the midweek Sabbath when we rest, we will have free time until dinner. I encourage you to exercise, journal, or as the Ignatians say, 'take a holy nap' during your free time."

Amy smiled. She'd never heard that phrase before and loved the idea of a holy nap. It was like receiving permission to rest. And for a girl used to running herself ragged, rest sounded like heaven.

"After dinner we will have another practice, a triad time, and end the evening at nine with the examen in the chapel. You can also join the monks at the various times when they pray. In your rooms, you can find a list of those prayer times and the other embodied prayers that are listed in the welcome packet."

Amy had no idea what Tom meant about "joining the monks" and "embodied prayer" but made a mental note to read about it later. Tom turned on the projector for a PowerPoint presentation He began talking about how after Jesus left, some people called "desert fathers and mothers" went into the desert and lived as monks, practicing silence, stillness, and solitude.

This led to the monastic movement where people lived together and followed rules of order. These became orders of priests and nuns, like the Benedictines, who were hosting them. He went on listing names and dates, but what struck Amy was when he said, "When the Reformation came, a lot of great changes happened in the church, but unfortunately, the baby was thrown out with the bathwater. The Protestants kept Bible study and more symbolic forms of prayer that involved language, as in praying spontaneously out loud, and the Catholics kept the more mystical prayer practices, some of which we will be trying this week. Most of them became inaccessible to Catholics, as well, as they were used mostly by monks in monasteries. It was as if a great wall divided the Catholics and the Protestants.

"In the seventies, people began to practice some of these ancient forms of prayer, and the Protestant church labeled them 'New Age.' But the truth is the Christian tradition has a wonderful legacy of these practices; they've just been hidden away until recently. We live in a fantastic time." Tom's face became very animated as he spoke. "The giant wall that separated the Catholic Church from the Protestant church has become a low hedge that we can easily step back and forth over. The Catholics are asking the Protestants to teach them how to study the Bible and the Protestants are asking the Catholics to teach them to pray. It's a great time to be alive."

Amy thought about that. It made sense. In her evangelical background, Catholics had always been held at arm's length. She'd even heard them referred to as part of a cult. But Amy was ready for some new way to talk to God. Her rote prayer lists were wearing thin. She needed some new ways to pray. She was done with prayers that weren't making a difference. Amy noticed her Muslim friend Amani whisper something to Felicia and leave the room. Was this too much talk about Christianity for her? Amy worried about how she was taking this retreat and had to force herself not to run out after her to be sure she was okay.

Tom continued. "The practice we will try now is called Lectio Divina. In Latin it means holy reading. You will be letting the scripture read you. I'll read the passage slowly three times. The first time just listen. The second time, listen for a word or phrase that stands out to you and repeat it over and over in your mind. Then we'll have some time to speak that word or phrase out loud. I'll read the passage a third time and you'll listen for an invitation from the passage, which we will share in our triads. Don't worry; I'll prompt you before each reading.

"Now, relax back into your chair and begin your conscious breathing."

5

It took a while for Amy's triad, which was actually made up of four members, to find each other. They settled their chairs into a square pattern next to a large window facing out onto the lake. To her right sat a South Asian woman who said her name was Hasmita. Her black hair was pulled to the front in a braid that hung down to her lap, and she wore a beautiful blue sari. Next to her, across from Amy, was a gorgeous man about her age with sandy-blond hair and a tall, husky frame. Perfect, of course—he was even wearing a 49ers T-shirt. There was only one problem: the ring on his left hand. Why were the best ones always married?

To Amy's left was a blond woman in her late thirties or early forties who introduced herself as Connie. She had a cute, shoulder-length layered hairdo, but her eyes looked lined and weary. She spoke first. "I'm from Branson, Missouri. I have two daughters, five and seven, and work in a hospice as the volunteer coordinator." Hospice—Amy wondered if that accounted for the weary look. Working with people who were dying had to be exhausting.

The beautiful boy went next. Amy tried to keep her mind off his lips and on his words. "As I said, I'm Stephen. I live in San Jose and work for a tech start-up in the Silicon Valley . . . and"—he glanced down as if unsure—"I'm part of a church plant there."

Amy noticed that he didn't mention his wife. Connie hadn't mentioned a husband either, but she wasn't wearing a ring. He turned to Hasmita.

"I am from Denver, Colorado," she said in a crisp accent that enunciated each syllable. "I work at a refugee center there. I am not married, much to my family's disappointment. The rest of my family lives in India."

"You must miss them," said Stephen.

"Yes I do, very much," agreed Hasmita, then turned to Amy.

"I'm from Reno, Nevada. I'm going to graduate school for social work." She figured that was all they really needed to know, so she moved on. "And we are supposed to share about the Lectio Divina. I've never done that before, even though I've heard that passage about Jesus healing blind Bartimaeus several times. It gave the passage a whole new meaning for me." She remembered how whenever they'd studied that passage with the high school youth group that she and Joshua led, he'd called the main character of the story Blind Bart. She could see Joshua standing up, his whole body tense with excitement as he told the story. It was his enthusiasm that made him such a great youth leader. The kids loved him. Oh, how she wished Joshua were here, or Jennie—someone who knew her.

Her group mates waited for her to go on. She thought about the exercise. The first time they'd just listened to the story about Jesus going up the road in a crowd when a man who'd been born blind started calling out, "Jesus, Son of David, have mercy on me!" People tried to shush the man, but he got louder. Finally, Jesus stopped and came over to talk to him.

Amy took a breath. "When Jesus said, 'What do you want me to do for you?' that's the part that stuck in my head. I let that question roll over and over in my mind after the second reading. Then in the third reading, when we were supposed to listen for the invitation from the passage—well, I felt like that was the most important question for me this week. I really don't even begin to know how to answer that. I don't know what I need God to do for me. We've not exactly been on . . . speaking terms lately. Well, that's not exactly true. I'm not mad at God, just—his people." She held her breath, waiting for the platitudes and advice she was sure would come.

Surprisingly, she saw no judgment from her group mates. In fact, both Stephen and Connie had nodded as if understanding. She sat back in her chair and looked at her lap.

Connie spoke up. "I thoroughly relate to that, Amy. Although I *am* pretty mad at God. I spent most of the exercise battling cynical thoughts, and I wasn't really able to get past them. So, sorry, guys—I've got nothing." Amy was grateful for her honesty.

"No harm, no foul," said Stephen, nodding. Then he was quiet as if thinking. "I related mostly to Bartimaeus. I feel blind right now. Can't see. I guess I've not been calling out much for help, just trying to figure it out on my own. So, I guess that is my hope for this week—to get some clarity for my life." He nodded again, then looked at Hasmita.

"I'm Hindu," she said. "This was my first time really listening to a story about Jesus. I was struck by his compassion. He stopped to talk to what we would consider an untouchable. I thought about how I judge people and how I need to see past the social barriers to the heart of the people."

Amy felt chastised by Hasmita's words, although she knew they were not shared to make her feel guilty. It just seemed that Hasmita, a Hindu, had a much better handle on what was really important to God than Amy did as a Christian.

Connie spoke up. "I don't mean to be rude, but I need to run to my room before lunch. I'll catch you all later tonight."

With that, the group broke up, and Amy was a little disappointed. She wanted to learn more about her group mates. She had always loved learning about people. That's one thing she liked about her master's degree. They talked a lot about what made people tick. At least her curiosity hadn't died. She wandered outside to soak up some warmth until lunch. She found a chair facing the lake and propped her feet up on the cement wall that encircled it. Their first night on retreat, Tom had offered a basket for them to put their phones in if they wanted to be disconnected from technology during the retreat. She didn't think she would have survived that. She decided to spend the break texting Joshua.

AMY: I wish you were here. You wouldn't believe the jokes I've wanted to share with you already.

JOSHUA: I wish I were too, instead of making Frappuccinos for friggin' idiots.

AMY: Rough day at the office?

JOSHUA: This guy practically threw his coffee at me because I put whip on it. I KNOW he said whip! A-hole. I should have spit in his cup.

Amy laughed.

AMY: Sorry. You on break?

JOSHUA: No, it's just slowed down, but I should go. You okay?

AMY: Yeah, but pray for my attitude. I'm fighting the urge to steal a car and run away!

JOSHUA: Will do. Hang in there, baby. You know there has to be a reason you're in the cornfields.

AMY: So I can be killed by the Children of the Corn?

JOSHUA: Ahhh, no. Why did you say that? You know that movie gave me nightmares for years. Now I'll worry about you.

AMY: I'll be fine. Well, I'll let you go.

JOSHUA: Yeah, customers heading this way.

AMY: Give my love to Petie!

JOSHUA: The Petester sends his love. I'll write back later. Bye.

She slid her phone into her back pocket.

She pictured Joshua working at the Starbucks counter, a place he thought he was done with when he'd gotten the job at the big church they'd grown up in. He, too, had been fired from the church, which was a shame because he was hands down the best youth leader the church had ever had. But then there was Peter. Peter had slipped into Joshua's heart. Suddenly it was as if Joshua's lifetime of faithfulness to the church and to God counted for nothing. When he'd told the board of his decision to date Peter, he'd been asked to resign immediately. Amy's face heated at the memory and her eyes flooded with tears. Horrible, awful words had been said that day as they sat around the conference table. Three pastors, six elders, one of them being her dad, and she and Joshua. Words like *abomination* and *degenerate* had flown from the lips of people Amy had respected all her life. The accusations flew like bile from their mouths. Her father sat there, silent. Silent! Joshua had been like a son to him and he'd done nothing. Joshua had been crushed and Amy stunned. Surely they couldn't mean it. Joshua had always been gay. Nothing had changed except that he'd fallen in love. She shook her head, trying to shake off the memory. Everything had changed that day, for both of them.

6

Amy sat with Brooke and Natalie at lunch and was sad to hear they were skipping the one o'clock special topic of the day. Maybe she should skip it.

"I took a whole Enneagram class in college," said Natalie, her doe eyes widening as she blew on a spoonful of tomato soup. "You'll love it!" Amy had never even heard of the Enneagram until she had taken the online test as directed on the conference registration site, but her results were unclear at best.

Brooke agreed. "We used it at the church where I got fired. It was the best part of working there, actually." Amy laughed at that. Brooke had a very disarming way about her. She was able to be real about hard things without bitterness.

Natalie leaned forward, whispering. "Brooke and I are cooking up a little mischief for later. Would you be interested in a possible *outing* sometime soon?"

Amy smiled. "Would I? I've already been contemplating ways to escape."

Natalie smiled and raised her eyebrows, looking at her watch. "Time to go, but we'll keep you posted. The plans—they are afoot!"

That thought, even though she had no clue what they were planning, gave Amy great hope. Before lunch, she'd been contemplating skipping the special session, but now she felt energized.

After she finished her food Amy walked into the meeting room without her friends. The chairs were still in the big circle from the first session. She saw an open spot next to a middle-aged lady in capris and a flowered shirt but noticed her sandals and veered off to another seat. The sandals were bronze with large fake jewels set into the straps, and the lady's toenails were a sparkly red. She sat instead next to a guy with a hipster beard, waiting for the room to fill and wondering what it was about those sandals that made her veer away. She looked around the room at the feet of the people seated in the circle. Most wore plain sandals or slip-on canvas shoes like she did. She liked this brand because for every pair you bought, a pair was donated to a child who needed it. *I guess in a room full of activists, that lady's sandals look out of place. Like, there is a dress code for activism and she's not wearing it. What could I possibly have in common with her? I mean, she can afford a pedicure!* Then Amy remembered what Hasmita had said during their triad time. *Am I being judgmental?*

Amy's self-reflection was cut short when Felicia came into the room. "Why don't we pull the chairs up here in front of the Power-Point so we're not so spread out?"

Amy joined the others in pulling their chairs from the wide circle into loose rows at the front of the room. This class was attended by about two-thirds of the retreatants. She figured that the others, like her friends, were already familiar with the Enneagram.

Felicia started with the history of the Enneagram, which was not just a personality test but an ancient tool for growing from your "false self" into your "true self." Amy pondered that. What was her false self? The Enneagram looked a bit like a pentagram, but Felicia said it was made of interlocking triangles. She continued through all nine numbers on the points of the Enneagram star, describing the attributes of each. Some were easy for Amy to rule out. Her test had said she was either a two, three, or seven. As Felicia explained each number in detail, Amy narrowed her choices to the number two or the number three.

The two was described as the Helper or the Giver. It was someone who always wanted to be helpful, and Amy was definitely motivated to help others. The words that described the number two included generous, empathetic, warm, and sincere. She liked that. But the three, called the Achiever, was driven to perform. She'd been in all the plays in high school. She loved performing, public speaking, and any opportunity to lead from up front, which is why she'd loved her job as the outreach director at church. Words that described the three were charming, ambitious, competent, and energetic. These were words that would describe her too. She was still confused.

"The proof," said Felicia, "is when you find the dark, or shadow, side of your number. You'll know you've found the right number if you absolutely *hate* the description of your number's shadow."

Amy looked down at the handout she'd been given. For the number two, it said their shadow side involved being "over helpful" in order to get praise. That they would even manipulate others with their helpfulness to get their own needs for affirmation met. They could become martyrs to help others, but their help was often motivated by a fear of worthlessness. Amy didn't like the sound of that at all. Surely, she was not like that.

The shadow side of the three was that they worked so hard to please others, and perform for others, they forgot to take care of themselves until they didn't really know who they were anymore. *Hmm*, thought Amy. Did she know who she was anymore? Had she thought she was "doing the right thing" to please God, or her parents, or her own confused values? Had she worked so hard she'd lost herself?

To make matters even more confusing, Felicia said you had a dominant wing, a number to one side of your number that you would "lean into." It would be a large part of your personality. So, if Amy was a two, she would lean into a one or a three. A one was a perfectionist. She definitely didn't lean that way. One look at her bedroom would tell you that—heck, one look at her room here at the monastery would tell you that. It was covered with her clothes draped on every possible surface. She could be a two that leaned into the three. That made sense. A giver that leaned into performing.

If she was a three, she could lean into the two. That made sense too. Or she could lean into a four. A four was considered a romantic, artistic person. Hmm—she didn't really think so. She concluded, *I am either a two with a three wing or a three with a two wing.*

As the class ended and people started putting the chairs back, Amy walked up to Felicia, who was stacking up her papers. She pushed back the strong pull she was feeling that she should be helping with the chairs, but she really wanted answers. "Felicia, I feel stuck between a two and a three. How do I figure it out?"

"Give yourself some time to mull it over. Or ask people that know you. Remember, if you really hate the shadow side, it's probably a good indication of your number. The goal is to learn to acknowledge the shadow side, not beat ourselves up over it. If we can own it, we can begin to live more into our true self."

"Thanks," said Amy, thinking that Felicia's explanation was about as clear as the overcast sky. She left the room and exited through the large glass doors to the muggy afternoon. She knew just who to ask. She sat on one of the white plastic chairs that ringed the building side of the lake and pulled out her phone to text Joshua.

AMY: Have I ever been "overly helpful" to you?
JOSHUA: Huh?
AMY: We did this Enneagram personality thing, and the number that I might be says I like to be helpful, but the down side is that I can be overly helpful, like when people aren't asking for my help.
JOSHUA: Uh, yeah . . . I can see that.

Anger flared up Amy's spine.

AMY: WHAT? What do you mean? Give me an example.

JOSHUA: Hey, you asked. Don't get mad at me.

AMY: Sorry . . . I really do want to know.

AMY: Sort of.

JOSHUA: You SURE?

AMY: Yes.

JOSHUA: Okay, here goes.

JOSHUA: Like when we took those kids to Mexico to build houses and you took over, ordering everyone's food like you were our mom.

Amy remembered that. They were all tired and stressed and she thought she was being . . . helpful. Her stomach sank.

JOSHUA: And that time I broke my arm and you brought me meals every day for a month.

AMY: I thought you liked that.

Now she was feeling hurt. Had she been doing things for people that they didn't want her to do?

JOSHUA: I did, but every day? For a month? It got a bit overwhelming.

AMY: Why didn't you tell me?

JOSHUA: I didn't want to hurt your feelings. You seemed to get so much joy out of doing it.

Amy sat with her thumbs hovering over her phone. He was protecting her because he didn't want to hurt her feelings, because she was trying to serve him, but . . . doing it so she'd feel good? She felt sick to her stomach.

AMY: I think I'll go lie down now.

JOSHUA: Ammmmmyyyy. You can't leave like that. Are we okay? I didn't mean to hurt your feelings. You asked!

AMY: No. No worries. We're good. I just need to process this a bit more.

JOSHUA: You sure? I love you.

AMY: I love you too. We're good.

Amy slowly rose from her chair and walked to the building. She pulled open the door and a cool air-conditioned blast assaulted her. She headed down the hall to her room, hoping no one would speak to her. It was as if each step drained the energy from her body. Opening her door, she flipped off her shoes and flopped facedown on her bed. She pretty much thought everyone liked her. Did they really see her as bossy and overly helpful? Was she doing things to help others with a secret fear that if she didn't, she was worthless and needed affirmation?

Now that she saw it, she couldn't unsee it. The desire to make a food run for Amani, her desire to follow her out of the room and be sure she was okay . . . Tears began to soak her pillow until sobs shook her frame. There would be no afternoon yoga for her today. In fact, she felt so bad, so worthless, so stupid, that she might never leave this room again.

7

A knock on the door jolted her awake. Amy sat up on her bed, disoriented. The light in the room was dim—was it morning? She shuffled to the door and pulled it open. Natalie and Brooke stood there, looking concerned.

"We missed you at afternoon yoga; then when you didn't come for dinner, we thought we'd better check on you," said Natalie.

"It's a good thing too," said Brooke, pushing past Amy into the room. "You look like crap."

Natalie followed Brooke into the room and turned on a light. Amy squinted at the brightness and closed the door. The girls stood, looking for a place to sit. "Sorry—just push something over and have a seat."

"We brought you some food," said Natalie, pulling a banana and a napkin with cookies from her pockets and handing them to Amy. Brooke pushed all of the clothes to one side of the unused bed and sat down; Natalie sat next to her. Amy plopped down across from them on her own bed.

"So, spill," said Brooke. "What's wrong?"

Amy felt heat rush to her face. "I feel stupid. I just got really upset over the Enneagram." Surprisingly she saw Natalie and Brooke nod in understanding.

"What number are you?" asked Natalie. "I'm a nine and I was really upset when I figured it out. We have trouble making decisions and knowing our own minds."

"I'm a two," said Amy, discouraged. "We tend to be overly helpful. Only, I never saw it that way, until today."

"Well," laughed Brooke, "I'm an eight—most people hate me!"

Amy smiled. Felicia said the eight was a strong personality, like a bull in a china shop, but had a huge heart for justice. In fact, it was the dark side of the eight that Amy's two went to when she was stressed, and it was why she became bossy. Yikes. To have to deal with that constantly must be difficult. She peeled her banana and took a big bite.

"Don't worry about it," said Brooke. "The point of the Ennea-gram is to make you aware of your shadow side so you can be mindful of it and grow toward the light side. Let me see your handout."

Amy remembered thinking these two girls were young and naive, but it turned out they had more wisdom than she did. Amy looked around the room. She'd dropped her bag with the handout onto the floor when she'd walked in. She grabbed it now, pulling it onto the bed and yanking out the stapled papers.

Brooke grabbed it out of her hand. "Look, when you're stressed, you go to the low side of the eight—lucky you, and wel-come to my life. But when you're happy, you go to the high side of the four. It says a four's high side is romantic and creative. What do you like to do that's romantic and creative?"

Amy thought about that. "Nothing romantic—unfortunately." Her heart sank. "I was kind of dumped by my almost fiancé a few months ago, and now he's engaged to someone else."

"Oh no," said Natalie.

"His loss," said Brooke.

Amy smiled. "I used to do theater. I loved acting when I was little, and I used to do skits for the high school group at church with my friend Joshua. But . . . nothing lately."

"That's what you need to think about," said Brooke. "How do you add creativity back into your life—and romance too!" Her eyebrows shot up and down suggestively.

Amy pulled her notebook out of her bag and began writing.

"What's that?" asked Natalie.

Amy held the notebook up for the girls to see. "It's my 'thirty things to do before I turn thirty' list."

Brooke grabbed the notebook from her hand. "One: lose ten pounds. Two: start taking yoga. Three: do something creative. This list needs some work!" She handed the notebook back to Amy. "Add 'create an online dating profile.'"

Amy grimaced. "Do I have to? I tried that." She shivered and said in the voice of a moron, "Hey beautiful, heaven called; they're missing an angel."

Natalie laughed. "I tried too. The Christian ones are just as bad! 'Are you religious? 'Cause you're the answer to all my prayers.'" Brooke snorted and Amy laughed. She was starting to feel better and glad that her friends had come to find her.

"Yes," said Brooke. "But you don't need to fall in love. Just go on dates. How else will you find out what you could live with and what you definitely don't want to live with!"

Natalie nodded reluctantly.

Brooke grabbed the notebook back and a pen and wrote, "Four: go on ten dates." She looked up. "Otherwise, how will you ever have any romance in your life? You need romance!" She tapped the pen on the paper. "We wanted to tell you to meet us in the parking lot after the examen tonight. We're going to town to have a beer. Bring your list and we'll work on it some more."

Amy nodded as if this was the most natural idea; though going out for a beer was not something she'd ever really done before. To keep from speaking, she bit into the chocolate chip cookie. She was hungry and grateful for these friends who seemed . . . real.

"We'd better go," said Natalie. "It's time for the evening meeting."

Amy grabbed her bag, shoving the notebook into it, and followed the girls out of the door. She was so glad they'd come looking for her. She didn't feel so awful now, but she might have gotten stuck in that dark place if they hadn't stopped by.

The fluorescent lights in the main room felt too bright for Amy. She realized she'd neglected to look in the mirror and tried to smooth her hair, wondering if her eyes were puffy from crying.

Tom greeted them and led them in a "be still and know that I am God" breath prayer. The topic of the night was centering prayer.

"Centering prayer is another way to enter into silence, solitude, and stillness. Each of these teaches us its opposite. Silence teaches us to listen, solitude teaches us to be fully present with others, and stillness teaches us discerning action."

Amy liked to listen when Tom talked. He had such a fresh way of explaining things. She wondered if there were other men like him in the world. Single ones.

He continued. "As several of us discussed in the Enneagram training today, our unconscious motivations keep us busy in order to mask our underlying pain."

What underlying pain were her unconscious motivations masking? She needed to think about that more.

"As we surrender to silence, solitude, and stillness, we develop the capacity to know who we are. Why we are here. What we are supposed to give our time and energy to."

Amy really, really wanted the answers to those questions. She was learning a lot in her master's degree but still did not feel a pull to any particular thing. She had to learn this silence, solitude, and stillness thing if it would help her find those answers.

"Centering prayer is the practice of sitting quietly for twenty minutes, twice a day."

Amy didn't think that sounded too hard.

"The goal is to sit in the presences of the Divine and consent to the presence and action of God in you. Your mind will stray, so you can choose an anchor word, a holy word, to draw you back to the present. Some people picture a stream floating by and when thoughts come, you place them on a leaf and float them down the river. Chose a way that works for you. Let's try it. Find your sit bones and be mindful of your breathing."

Amy settled into a comfortable position and tried to picture herself sitting by a gentle river. As Tom rang the gong, she sat quietly. Her stomach grumbled—she remembered missing dinner and wished she'd hidden away some snacks. *Oops, put that on a leaf and send it down the river.* She breathed deeply. Her leg itched. She remembered that she was going out tonight with the girls . . . that would be—*uh-oh, on a leaf down the river.* The thoughts came and went and Amy put them on leaves and sent them down the river, sure that she was doing this all wrong. It sounded easy, but her brain felt like it was full of a tangle of unending thoughts, and her river was getting totally backed up with leaves.

8

After the contemplative practice, it was triad time, and Amy joined her group by the windows. Centering prayer had been a disaster for her, as she was never able to calm her mind, but Tom said it took practice. She looked forward to this group time because Tom's instructions had been intriguing "Each of you is here for a different reason. Most of you, because of the nature of activism, of doing good work, need to share some of the difficult things you've experienced. Tonight I want you to share what it is that needs healing or where you feel stuck. We will do this every night so each of you gets a whole night to share, but if you have four members, you'll have to let two people share on one night. Either way, don't rush. Take your time. Be as open and honest as you can." Tom cupped his hands like he was trying to hold water and said, "At the end of each person's sharing, take one minute of silence to just hold each person's story in the presence of the Divine."

Amy wondered if she was ready to share. What would she say? She needn't have worried. As soon as they sat down, the perfectly coiffed Connie spoke up. "I'd like to go first. It might help me to get some of this out." She paused, and when no one argued, she continued. "The reason I'm here is, like you, Amy, someone paid my way." Amy smiled at that. Who knew she wasn't the only one.

Connie took a deep breath. "I had some friends who were worried about me and sent me here. That's how it felt, like an intervention or a jail sentence.

"I told you I was mad at God. I'm not sure I want to be a Christian anymore, and the reason is I was married to a pastor." Amy laughed nervously; she knew that life in the fishbowl of ministry, where everyone thought the pastor's life should be theirs to critique, could be a pain. Connie gave her a weak smile and began to speak slowly, her words picking up speed as her story unfolded. "From the outside we looked like the perfect family. No one knew what was going on inside our marriage. We have two beautiful daughters; I'll never regret that. But I regret everything else. He—John—became increasingly controlling as the years went by. He gave me an allowance, he wouldn't let me spend time with my friends, but he had all the time in the world for the other women in our church." Her voice took on a harsh edge.

Amy felt so sorry for Connie. She had judged her as looking like she had it all together; now she was hearing incredible pain. Who knew what people were living with? Amy kicked off her shoes and tucked her legs up under her.

Connie took a breath and continued. "He started to yell at me if I gained weight and wouldn't let me leave the house if my hair wasn't perfect or if I didn't have on makeup."

Amy's heart broke. "That's emotional abuse," she said.

"I know," said Connie. "We went to see a *Christian* counselor." She emphasized the word Christian with finger quotes. "The counselor said I just needed to submit and work harder." A tear slid down Connie's cheek and she swiped at it with her sleeve.

Stephen sucked in a breath, looking as angry as Amy felt.

Amy wanted to punch someone—that counselor for sure, and Connie's ex. This was ridiculous. It sounded like a story from the fifties, not now. But the story got worse.

"At the same time, things weren't going well at church. John had a disagreement with the pastor and it blew up into a big thing. John actually got a bunch of people on his side and left the church. He started a new church, which was, in retrospect, more of a personality cult. People thought John could do no wrong. I mean, he had a heart for the homeless and was great with the kid's ministry. But with me he was awful."

"Aghhh!" said Stephen, digging his hands through his hair like he wanted to pull it out.

The women laughed. Amy was glad she wasn't the only one feeling violent.

"The church was becoming very cult-like," said Connie. "I tried to talk to the elders, but they thought it was my problem, because they thought John walked on water. I finally took the girls and left one day after John had gone to work. I had nothing—no money, nowhere to live, no job training. It was very hard. But it was the best day of my life."

"Where did you go?" asked Hasmita. "What did you do for food?"

Connie smiled with trembling lips. "My parents helped us. Sadly, I lost most of my friends when I left John. Because *I* was the one who left."

Amy was familiar with that phenomenon. In the evangelical church, you were not supposed to get divorced. "God hates divorce" was a passage she'd heard quoted time and time again. No matter what one person did—lying, cheating, gambling—it was usually the person who left the marriage that got cut off from the fellowship.

"I've been bitter and angry at God for letting this happen," said Connie. "But as far as my life goes, I'm so happy to be rid of John." She sat back in her chair as if finished.

"That is an amazing story," said Amy. "You are incredibly brave."

"Yes," agreed Stephen and Hasmita.

"Thank you," said Connie, her eyes glistening. "So you can see why I have issues. But that's where I'm at." They all nodded. Silence stretched out.

"Let's hold Connie's story," said Stephen.

The group fell silent and Amy opened her hands like a cup, the way Tom had, picturing Connie and her girls and all they'd been through inside her hands, in the presence of the Divine.

After some time, Hasmita spoke up. "Connie, your story gives me courage to tell my own story. As you know, I am a teacher of refugee children. According to my culture, I am too old not to be married. My friends talked me into using an online dating app, and it was there I met a wonderful Hindu man. What I am going to tell you now is very embarrassing to me." Amy nodded to encourage her.

"I should have seen it." Hasmita shook her head. "But you must understand how attentive he was. Every day he sent me pictures; every day he wrote me poems. He lived in India, so we had not met in person, and he told me that his computer's camera was broken so that we could not Skype, but we talked on the phone all the time."

Amy wondered where this story was going. Would it make her rethink the idea of adding "creating an online dating profile" to her list? She uncrossed her legs and sat up.

"I feel so embarrassed," Hasmita said again, "but you must understand. He talked to my roommate, he called my mother on Mother's Day, and he even sent my father a birthday card. We were all fooled. When he proposed, I said yes." She shook her head and chuckled. "I even had a little bachelorette party with my friends.

"When I went home this summer, we were to meet in person. He was coming to meet my family before we were to be married. But on the day he was to come, he didn't arrive. When I tried to call him, I discovered his phone had been disconnected. Of course, I worried that he had been in an accident."

Amy wondered why Hasmita's fiancé had gone to all that trouble but then not shown up. Had he died?

"My sister is very tech savvy. When we hadn't heard from him, she went on Facebook and found that he had blocked me. Then she typed his name into the computer, without using his middle initial, and found that it was the same name as an up-and-coming Indian actor. All of the pictures he'd been sending me were pictures of that actor."

"Wait, what?" said Amy. "I don't get it."

Connie explained. "He was using the actor's pictures to create a fake persona, right? They call it being catfished."

"Yes," said Hasmita. "And I never heard from him again. We did not tell my parents this, just that the marriage was off."

"Was he trying to get money from you?" asked Stephen.

"That's the funny thing," said Hasmita. "He bought me gifts and sent pictures of them, saying he'd give them to me when we saw each other. I bought him gifts and he said, 'No, don't spend any money on me.' Then, right before I went home to meet him, he asked for some money—twelve hundred dollars for an investment opportunity. But sadly, I didn't have it to give him."

"It's a good thing you didn't have it," said Stephen, "but twelve hundred seems a small amount to go through all of that."

"I have a theory," said Hasmita. "That he was originally supposed to scam me. Then accidentally fell in love with me. Then, at the end, he tried to get some money after all. The whole thing is so embarrassing."

The other three members rushed to assure Hasmita that she needn't be embarrassed; anyone would have been fooled by a con like that.

As they held Hasmita's story, Amy felt like maybe her problems weren't so bad after all. It seemed everyone had difficulties in their lives and she needed to stop judging people by the way they looked.

9

Amy felt gleeful piling into the back seat of Natalie's Toyota. Her stomach felt like she'd taken a dip on a roller coaster, like she was doing something wrong, sneaking out or something. Brooke sighed heavily as they pulled out of the parking lot in the dark. "Jeez, it feels like we've been here a week and it's only been two days."

Amy agreed. "Not even two days—less than a day and a half. This is so intense! You wouldn't believe the stories I heard in my triad."

"Mine too," agreed Natalie. "By the way, where are we going?" She had pulled up to the main road, which was bordered by miles of cornfields and a few streetlights.

"Turn left," said Brooke. "I Googled pubs and there's not much open at this hour. But I found one seedy little bar about ten miles up the road, and I need a beer."

Amy smiled. She liked Brooke with her big voice and honest ways. She was refreshing. As Natalie drove, Brooke used her phone to help them navigate. Amy's phone buzzed.

JOSHUA: You still alive?
AMY: I survived the day; now headed to a bar with my new friends.
JOSHUA: A bar? You? You're at a conference in a monastery and now you're going to a bar? This I want to see.
AMY: Hahaha! I've been to a bar before.
JOSHUA: When?

Amy thought about it. Had she ever been to a bar? Her dad was an elder in their church and part of that role was a commitment not to drink, so they didn't keep alcohol in their home. At college she'd joined and quickly become a leader in a campus Christian group. Part of their leadership covenant was not to drink. Then she'd become a missionary in Thailand—same policy. She racked her brain. *Had* she ever been to a bar?

Her freshman year she and Jennie had ventured out to a frat party and had their first experience with Everclear. She found out later it was a tasteless, very strong form of alcohol that had been handed to her as a "wine cooler." She had to hold Jennie's hair back that night as she hugged the toilet. That had put her off alcohol.

Then it dawned on her and she typed:

AMY: Of course I've been in bars—all the time in Thailand!

JOSHUA: That doesn't count. Rescuing sex-trafficked girls from bars is not the same as going to a bar to drink. You *are* going to a bar to drink, aren't you?

AMY: I guess.

JOSHUA: Well, don't do anything I wouldn't do.

AMY: That leaves it wide open.

JOSHUA: Seriously, have fun, Pooh Bear.

AMY: I will. Good night, Tigger.

JOSHUA: Night.

It was as if a weight had been lifted off her shoulders talking to Joshua. She'd felt bad about their earlier conversation and was glad to reconnect. Hearing her nickname from him let her know there were no hard feelings. That's how Joshua was: quick to forgive.

Amy tucked her phone in her back pocket and noticed they'd come into a small town. Emphasis on *small*. She could see a gas station and a bail bonds building. That did not inspire confidence.

"There it is," said Brooke, pointing to a small white building lit by a single streetlight, with two cars out front. A crooked neon beer sign listed to one side next to a weathered wooden sign that read simply, "Joe's." Amy felt a shiver of fear run up her spine. Should they be going into this dive? Was it safe? Were there escaped cons around here?

Brooke seemed to think it was perfect and jumped out as soon as Natalie pulled into a parking space. "Come on, ladies—time's a-wasting."

Amy crawled out and followed Natalie and Brooke into the dark bar. Country music played and a bartender stood behind a long bar with stools in front of it that ran across the front of the room. It reminded Amy of something from a movie, the stereotype of a seedy bar. Two middle-aged men sat at the bar drinking beer, a pile of peanut shells on the counter between them. Brooke seemed quite at home and led them to one of the small tables with chairs in front of the windows that faced the street. The windows had a bubbled plastic tinting on them, so you really couldn't see much, which, Amy supposed, was the point.

The bartender came to their table, wiping his hands on his apron. Amy thought he was not at all like a stereotype. In movies, the bartenders were always good-looking, manly men, and this guy was short, balding, and had a paunch that made him look about seven months pregnant. "You ladies know what you want?" he asked.

Brooke said, "Do you have anything to eat?"

"Sorry. Kitchen's closed."

"Bummer," said Brooke. "I'm hungry." Amy's stomach growled in agreement. She had missed dinner and was feeling it.

"I could microwave some nachos. They're not great, just a little something I make for myself sometimes."

"Sold!" said Brooke.

"What can I get you to drink?" he asked as he flipped white paper coasters onto the wooden table with a map of Nebraska laminated under the varnish.

"What's on tap?" asked Brooke.

"Coors, Bud, and Nebraska's favorite, Boulevard Unfiltered Wheat."

"Oh, I'll try the Boulevard. When in Rome . . ." said Brooke like a pro. Then she turned to Amy.

"Um, I'm not sure. Is there a menu?"

"Yeah," said Natalie, "I'd like to see one."

The bartender lifted a rectangular card with ketchup stains from the center of the salt and pepper shakers and laid it on the table between Natalie and Amy. "I'll get your nachos and come back."

"What do you normally drink?" asked Brooke, looking at Amy.

"Diet Pepsi," said Amy. Brooke smiled, nodding. "I've had wine at weddings, and champagne. I don't like beer; it's too bitter. My Opa tried to get me to like it—I mean, what's a German without beer?—but I just don't."

"Not much experience drinking, then?" summarized Brooke.

"Nope," agreed Amy.

"Hand me that list of yours," said Brooke, gesturing to Amy's bag.

Amy pulled her notebook out and handed it to Brooke, who pulled the pen from the metal spiral spine and tapped it as she regarded the list. "I'm going to write something we can check off tonight," she said. She scribbled on the page and turned it to Amy and Natalie to read: "Five: get drunk."

"What?" Amy said, feeling like her eyes might pop from her head. "You can't just keep writing on my list. I have to agree."

"Well, if not drunk, then at least buzzed," said Brooke, revising number five. "Come on, Amy. You're almost thirty years old and when else will you have this safe of a place to experience an alcohol buzz?"

Amy glanced around at the bar. "*Safe?*" she asked.

"You're living in a monastery, for Christ's sake. There are no guys here to slip you a mickey." She pointed toward the two men at the bar. "And if those two try, Natalie and I have your back."

Natalie laughed and added, "You need to live a little, girl."

Amy finally grinned. Brooke was right—what safer place was there? She was in the middle of Nebraska cornfields. Who would know if she had a bit to drink? She'd always wanted to try it.

The bartender came back and sat down a huge pile of nachos and Brooke's beer. "What about you two?"

"I'll have the house white," said Natalie.

"And my friend here will have a White Russian," said Brooke without hesitation.

He left and Amy turned to Brooke, who was taking a huge bite of nachos. "What's in that?"

"Vodka, Kahlúa, and cream. It's tasty. Good for a first timer!" she said around her mouthful of chips.

Amy started shoveling chips in too. She knew drinking hard alcohol on an empty stomach wasn't a great idea. "I'd like to hear more about how you lost your job at the church."

Brooke leaned back in her chair and took a long sip of her beer, then belched, making both Natalie and Amy giggle. "Well, it's like this. I was hired on at this big church because the pastor wanted to reach the Millennials, who as we know have been leaving the church in droves. He loved my ideas of starting a ministry in a bar. We called it Faith on Tap."

"Wow," said Natalie. "That sounds fun."

"It was," said Brooke, pausing when the bartender reappeared with Natalie's wine and Amy's drink. Amy took a hesitant sip. It tasted pretty good. A warmth spread down her throat to her stomach. The second sip was even better.

"Like it?" asked Brooke.

"I do, actually," said Amy.

Brooke continued with her story. "I had fun thinking of a name. I thought of Scripture and Suds, Pub Theology . . . So anyway, the pastor loved the idea and even came a couple of times. It was pretty successful."

She shoved a cheesy chip in her mouth and leaned in, excitement lighting her features. "The rules were that you could ask any question, no holds barred. We wrote the questions and put them in an empty mug, then picked one each week to discuss. But, whatever your opinion on the topic, you had to start whatever you were going to say with, 'Currently I'm thinking . . .' Then you had to end whatever you said with, 'But I may be wrong.'"

"Now *that* is awesome!" said Natalie, raising her wine glass in a silent salute.

"I would love that," agreed Amy. "It would keep people from being so . . . argumentative."

"Shit yeah," said Brooke. "It was great."

Amy giggled. Was her head feeling lighter already? She grabbed her pen from the table, adding number six to the list.

"What did you write?" asked Natalie.

Amy felt heat in her face. Was it the drink or her embarrassment? "I need to learn how to swear."

Natalie and Brooke both laughed, and Amy had to laugh a bit too at the things on her list. She was struck by how good it felt to laugh and talk about these things.

"So what went wrong at the church?" she asked.

"It was the church ladies," said Brooke as she drained her beer and made a gesture to the bartender. A warm, pleasant sensation had taken over Amy's body, like all the stress she'd been feeling had leached away. She quickly ate a few more chips.

"At least, that's what it was at first. They never really said anything to me directly, but they would make these comments on my Facebook page that were . . . disapproving."

"Like what?" asked Natalie.

"Well, they didn't like anything about me. They didn't like my swearing, they didn't like my tattoos, they didn't like the way I dressed. I was pretty pissed after a while."

"How many tattoos do you have?" Amy asked in awe of Brooke.

"Currently five, but I plan to get more soon."

Natalie giggled. "I have five too."

Amy was surprised. Some of Brooke's tattoos were visible on her wrist and ankle, but none of Natalie's were. Now Natalie was staring at Amy. She took the pen and wrote, "Seven: get a tattoo."

Amy smiled, a bit lopsided. "I've actually been planning to get one. An edelweiss; it's a flower. I want it to honor my Opa, my grandfather."

"Why that flower?" asked Natalie.

"It was his favorite. He was in the mountain infantry of Germany, and they had them on their collars and caps. He said it was his good-luck charm." She sighed. "I miss him. He died in January."

"I'm sorry," said Natalie. "Mine died when I was ten. But I still have my grandma."

"Me too," said Amy. Then she remembered Brooke's story. "What about the pastor? Did he stand up for you?" The bartender came back and placed three more drinks on the table. Amy gulped. She was pretty sure she was already buzzed. She shoved more chips into her mouth.

"That's the thing," said Brooke. "I think he was jealous. He'd tried to start different things for the Millennials, but they never really took off. When the group started to grow, he tried to control it, saying that anyone who came also had to come to a Sunday service—that sort of thing. But the people who were coming were not people that wanted to go to church. That was the beauty of the whole thing. Some had been hurt in churches. Some had never even been to a church.

"Finally, I think I just pissed him off in a staff meeting and the next thing I knew I was told that 'giving was down' and they'd have to let me go."

"What did you say at the staff meeting to make him mad?" asked Natalie.

"A bunch of old, married white guys and me," said Brooke, "and them talking about their policy for celibacy for their unmarried volunteers and I said, 'I'm not sure I believe that anymore.' And they had a shit fit."

"You said that?" asked Natalie, her doe eyes growing even rounder.

"Mostly I just liked to get a rise out of them, but yeah, seriously, I'm thirty years old. I HAVE NEEDS." She said the last part so loud the men at the bar turned to look at them, and all three girls started giggling. The giggling turned to laughter, and they laughed so hard it was hard to stop. As soon as one would catch her breath, the giggles would start again, and Amy felt better than she had in a long time. Now she understood why people got addicted to alcohol—it made you feel invincible.

"But seriously," said Brooke. "I've been rethinking the 'wait till you're married' thing. I mean, it made sense in Bible times when women were married at thirteen, but I don't think they'd ever find themselves thirty and a virgin. It was a rule for another time."

Amy knew her eyes were huge. She'd never heard a Christian woman say something like that, especially someone she respected. She turned to Natalie. "What do you think?"

"I don't know. I was at a gathering with a bunch of young married women from my church and they were saying they wished they hadn't waited. Some felt like it was telling your body, 'Sex is bad,' for years, then getting married and telling yourself, 'Now it's okay.' Like, it's not that easy to turn off and on."

"Exactly," said Brooke. "I'm sick of middle-aged white men making up rules for me to live by. I'm going to start making my own rules based on my own relationship with God. No purity ring for this girl."

"I had a purity ring," said Amy sheepishly.

"Where is it?" asked Natalie.

"Well, you might not believe this, but I've never even kissed a guy."

"What?" said Brooke and Natalie together. Brooke made a grab for Amy's list and Amy pulled it away.

"Wait," she said. "Let me tell you. My dad took me out when I was twelve, after one of those parties the church has to celebrate celibacy, and he bought me the ring. I didn't want to disappoint him. I never had a boyfriend until West, and he and I decided that we shouldn't kiss till we got married, because he said it was too hard for him, so we never did. Then, after he broke up with me, I saw him kissing his new girlfriend in the church parking lot!"

"No way," said Natalie.

"Douche bag," said Brooke.

"So I drove right downtown and threw the purity ring off the bridge into the river."

"The river?" said Natalie, looking confused.

"We have this bridge in Reno, and back in the day, you could come to Reno for a quickie divorce. The women used to throw their rings right off that bridge. So that's what I did."

"So, you don't have your ring," observed Brooke, "but you still have your virginity."

"True," said Amy, her tongue feeling tingly. "But I'm not putting that on the list."

"Obviously," said Brooke.

"But you could put the kissing on the list," said Natalie.

"Yes," said Amy. "I will put the kissing on the list." She wrote, "Eight: kiss someone."

10

As they drove back to the monastery at midnight, Amy was feeling no pain. She barely noticed when Natalie drove the car past the entrance to the monastery guesthouse and kept going up the road, the headlights the only illumination on the now dirt road.

"Where are we going?" she said with words that seemed to come out slowly. Natalie and Brooke giggled. They were definitely plotting something.

"We wanted to help you take one more thing off your list tonight," said Natalie.

"Which one?" asked Amy as the car jerked to a stop and the girls in the front seat tumbled out. Amy opened her door. "I hope it's romance. Have you hidden a guy up here for me to kiss?" She was standing in the dirt in what looked like an orchard. Way down the hill, she could see the retreat center, lit up from the inside.

"Come on," said Brooke. "We're gonna teach you how to swear."

Amy stumbled up the hill into the trees behind her friends. Again her stomach felt the lurch of adventure. The night was cool but not cold and the stars were clustered above them, though a bit fuzzy to Amy's eyes.

Brooke stopped between two apple trees and turned to face the guesthouse far below. She put her hands on either side of her mouth like a megaphone and yelled, "FUCK!"

Amy started laughing. She had a hard time getting her breath she was laughing so hard. Was she really going to do this? She had just never been one to swear. Why had she put it on the list? It just seemed so funny and natural when Brooke did it.

Natalie stepped up to join Brooke and hollered in her high-pitched voice, "Shit, shit, shit!"

Amy clutched her sides, laughing again. This seemed so inappropriate. They were at a monastery! They were pretty far away, but what if the monks could hear them?

"Come on, Amy—it's your turn," said Brooke.

Amy stepped up to stand next to Brooke. She took a deep breath, put her hands to her mouth, and hollered, "Dammit!"

Now it was Brooke's and Natalie's turn to laugh. "You can do better than that," chided Brooke. "Let it fly. No one can hear you from here. Now's your chance."

Amy giggled, took a breath, and let an f-bomb fly. She had to admit it felt good. Soon all three were shouting expletives like kids at a Tourette's convention. Colorful words fell around them like rain until they were exhausted, sitting in the dirt and laughing. "I guess we'd better go to bed," said Brooke. "Breakfast comes early."

Amy realized the fresh air had sobered her up a bit. They climbed back into the car and Natalie carefully negotiated a three-point turn and began to slowly crawl down the dirt road.

"What's that?" said Natalie, slowing.

"Oh shit—it's somebody walking up this road," said Brooke.

Amy leaned forward in the seat to peer into the darkness. It didn't look like a monk. The headlights illuminated a tall guy wearing a sweatshirt and jeans. Then horror filled Amy. It was Stephen, from her triad. Natalie stopped the car and rolled down the window.

Stephen leaned his head down to see inside the car. "Ladies," he said in greeting. "Sounds like you're having a good evening."

"Sorry if we were too loud," said Natalie, giggling.

"Not a problem," he said, smiling back at Amy. "But Amy, someday I'd love to hear the story of this night!" He turned and continued his walk up the hill.

Amy flushed with embarrassment. "Oh my gosh. That guy is in my triad!"

"He's hot," said Natalie.

"Married," said Amy.

"Aren't they all," agreed Brooke. Soon they pulled into the retreat center parking lot and headed for the door.

Amy grabbed her friends' hands to stop them from going in, because once they were inside, they'd have to be quiet. "Thanks. I really needed a night like tonight. I can't remember when the last time was I've laughed so hard."

"Agreed," said Natalie.

"And seconded," said Brooke.

11

The next morning Amy awoke to her alarm, and the memories of the night before flooded over her. She was surprised she didn't feel hungover. When they'd dropped her off at her door, Brooke had whispered that she should take two Tylenol and drink a glass of water before bed. It was a preventative hangover cure. It must have worked.

She lay in her bed, grinning like a fool. She couldn't believe she'd stood over the monastery swearing. Her palm flew to her face—and Stephen had heard her. And she'd have to face him tonight in their triad. She was glad there hadn't been a tattoo parlor open; she'd have probably come back with a giant tattoo on her hip.

She crawled out of bed and pulled on her exercise clothes. She giggled again at the memories.

The morning had gone well with breakfast, yoga, and more teaching on desert mothers and fathers. Amy felt good today, lighter than she had in a long time. But her butt was numb from sitting and she decided to get a walk in before lunch.

The day was bright and warming nicely. She started around the lake and was trying to decide where to go next when a voice next to her said, "Can I join you?"

Amy was surprised to find the lady with the bronze sandals walking next to her. At first she cringed, again feeling that they would have nothing in common. But then she remembered her desire not to judge a person from the outside anymore. "Of course," she said.

"I'm Celeste," said the woman, who today was wearing black capris and a peasant top that could have come right out of a seventies fashion magazine. The same bronze flip-flops with large fake gems protected her pedicured feet.

"I'm Amy." As they exchanged pleasantries, Celeste led them off the paved path and stopped as they entered a trail made of mown grass surrounded by taller grasses a foot high.

"I was going to walk up to the stations of the cross. Is that okay with you?"

"Sure," said Amy. She didn't even know there were stations of the cross up here. In fact, she wasn't sure she knew what "stations of the cross" were.

"Well, you have to make friends with the grasshoppers if we go up there."

"What do you mean?" asked Amy.

"There are a lot of them right now, and they'll bounce off you, but they don't bite, of course."

"Okay," said Amy, wondering how hard it could be. She'd chased and caught plenty of grasshoppers in her youth. As they got farther up the path, clouds of two-inch-long grasshoppers puffed up with each of their footsteps. They bounced off Amy's arms and legs, whizzing by her face. "Wow, I'm glad you warned me."

"Yes, it's rather Old Testament, isn't it? At first I thought they were a swarm of locusts!"

Amy laughed as they continued to be bombarded by the beasts. They were quiet as they slogged up the hill. Amy liked the way Celeste said things. The phrases "make friends with the grasshoppers" and "it's rather Old Testament" rolled through her mind.

Celeste stopped at the crest of the hill and turned to Amy. "How is this retreat for you?" she asked. She had very nice eyes and a beautiful smile. Why hadn't Amy noticed that before instead of silently mocking the lady's sandals?

"Honestly, it's been pretty hard. That centering prayer was not working for me today, and my friend Natalie says she loves it. I must be doing it wrong."

Celeste laughed. It was a kind, musical sound. "I don't really get it either. It feels like monkeys are having a pillow fight in my head when I try to clear my brain."

Amy laughed hard at that. It was exactly how she felt. "Maybe if we keep practicing . . ."

"Maybe," agreed Celeste.

Celeste led them to the left and stopped at a skinny pole with a square picture on the top. "Here's the first station," she said.

Amy inspected it. The pole was made from silver rebar and embedded in a cross-shaped cement pad at its base. At the top, the rebar made a frame around a picture of Jesus being condemned to death. On the back it said, "Pray for those who are falsely accused and imprisoned for their faith."

"Hmm," said Amy.

"Have you prayed the stations before?" asked Celeste.

"No. I'm not sure I've really even seen them."

"They're interesting," said Celeste. "They look different in every church, of course. I think they were started for people who couldn't go on pilgrimage to Jerusalem; it's like going on a pilgrimage to walk with Jesus on his way to the cross, without having to leave town. And also, in a preliterate society, pictures like these and icons were a way to teach Bible stories and theology."

Amy added a new descriptor to her list of Celeste's attributes: she was smart! They wandered from station to station, pausing briefly to read each one and say a silent prayer. In between stations, they talked.

"Are you here with hurt from your life of advocacy, as Tom suggested?" asked Celeste as they left station six.

"I guess so," said Amy. "I didn't even know how burnt out I was until I got here. I feel so angry at the church. I just don't know what to do."

Celeste looked like she was considering Amy's statement. "I remember feeling the exact same way. It was when I had my mind map blown."

"Your what?"

Celeste stopped walking and turned to Amy. "We all have this understanding of God when we're young." She held her hands out in a circle. "And it's like our map of who God is." Then she moved her hands away from each other in a bigger circle. "Then something happens that blows out our mind map, and God gets so much bigger."

Amy let that soak in. Was that what was happening to her? Maybe God wasn't leaving her; maybe God was just getting bigger. Was her childhood understanding of God too small for her now? It was a little scary to think about.

Celeste continued. "I'll never forget the first time it happened. At least it was the first time I was aware of it. It was in the nineties, when I read this book about how the majority's understanding of Christ's return—you know, the Rapture and all that—was a relatively new idea. It has only been around about two hundred years. Before that, the common understanding was that Jesus would come back to the earth and restore his kingdom here. I felt really pissed off that I'd been a Christian twenty years and never heard that before. Do you see the difference it makes?"

Amy didn't. "I'm pretty sure everyone I know believes in the whole Rapture idea. You know, they fight about when Jesus will come back: pre-Tribulation, mid-Tribulation, or post-Tribulation. My dad's favorite joke is that he is a pan-Tribulationist. 'Whatever pans out, I'm gonna be there!'" she mimicked in her best Dad voice.

Celeste laughed. "Well, after I let it sink in, the idea that Jesus was coming back to restore the earth, then I realized we need to take care of the earth. He's not going to start over; he's coming to restore what we already have."

Amy liked that idea. She felt very close to God when she was in the trees and loved the biblical image that creation was waiting to be restored at Christ's return.

"Also," said Celeste, with her face getting more animated as she spoke, "it makes a difference how you think about evangelism. If Jesus is coming back here to stay, then we are not trying to rescue rats from a sinking ship, as I had been taught. But we get to love people here and now into the kingdom that has already arrived. The kingdom that will continue to be here after Christ's return! It's a much more loving, long-term perspective if you ask me.

"Anyway, that was just the start of it. Then I read a book about different views of the atonement, different models of the Christ— it just keeps going!"

If Amy's mind map was being blown this week, she was pretty sure it was being shattered to pieces. She saw Celeste glance at her watch and realized it was time for lunch. "Celeste, could I have lunch with you? I have more questions."

"Of course," Celeste said with a smile as they turned and headed down the hill, grasshoppers flying around them. "By the way, Amy, if you get a chance, there is a labyrinth on the back side of the monastery that's pretty cool."

"What's a labyrinth? Is it like a maze?"

Celeste laughed. "Sort of, but there is only one way in and out, so you can't get lost. And it's a path on the ground, so you can see the whole thing at once. You walk into it with prayer, like you can maybe pray out all the things you're angry about on the way in. Then in the middle is where you stop and rest in God's presence. I like to stand there a bit and just picture leaving all my concerns there. Then on the way out, I usually think of all the things I have to be grateful for."

Amy definitely wanted to find that labyrinth before she left this place, and she only had a few days left. They were on the path by the lake now, heading into the building. As they went through the doors, the air-conditioning wafted over them. "How do you know so much about the grounds?"

"Oh, I'm on sabbatical," said Celeste. "I came a week early and have been exploring."

"Sabbatical from what? Are you a professor?"

"No, I'm a pastor," said Celeste.

Amy had never met a female pastor, but she'd always been suspicious of them. Why was that, anyway? Celeste was so easy to talk to and she was spiritually like an ocean of depth. Amy would love to have a pastor like her.

"What denomination are you with?" Amy wondered if maybe she should be looking for a new church when she got home.

"It's called the Disciples of Christ. An old, but relatively small denomination."

They got in line for lunch and listened to the happy banter around them. She saw Natalie ahead in line, talking to Tom, and Brooke was behind her, talking to a small crowd of women. It was probably good that they branched out and met other people while they were here. She turned to Celeste, a sudden desire to confide coming over her—what did she have to lose? "I'm really mad at my church right now. I may be looking for a new one."

Celeste said nothing but waited for Amy to continue. "You see, my best friend, Joshua, is gay, and he was our church's high school youth leader. When he decided to date someone, a male, they asked him to leave. When I stood by him, I was asked to leave too." Amy was surprised when her eyes filled with tears. It was all still so fresh.

They were at the front of the food line, and Celeste put a hand on Amy's arm. "Let's get our food. We have more in common than you'd think."

12

Amy and Celeste settled in a small corner of the dining hall where they could have some privacy. As they sat down, Celeste said, "Now, tell me the whole story." Amy did, the words rushing from her. About coming home from the mission field, getting her dream job at the church, loving working with her best friend, and then how it all fell apart. All the while Celeste nodded and asked clarifying questions. It felt so good to be listened to, and Amy felt no judgment from Celeste. "And one of the hardest parts is that my folks are still there—they haven't left the church. My dad is an elder! They don't say it, but I feel like they think I've fallen away from my faith, if you know what I mean."

Celeste laughed, her green eyes sparkling. "I've been accused of that myself. You can't believe the number of times I've heard the phrase 'slippery slope.'"

"So, you said we had things in common. Can you say more?"

Celeste sipped her coffee. "Amy, I come from the same place you did. The evangelical church was my tribe. But I began to feel, around the eighties, like my tribe was leaving me. Everything became so political and the moral majority was formed . . . Suddenly Christianity became equated with conservative politics. Well, it was all before your time, but as I said, I felt like my tribe had left me, though I stayed in my church. Then, about ten years ago, my son came out to us as gay. We were heartbroken." She paused to sip her coffee.

Amy got it now, why Celeste seemed to understand. She had a gay son.

"At first, we tried to 'pray the gay away.' We sent Derek to counseling—reparative therapy they called it . . . I feel so bad about it now. Back then they blamed an 'overprotective mother' and a 'distant father.' There was a lot of guilt to work through. But Derek hadn't been sexually abused, he had a good relationship with his dad, and I wasn't like the helicopter moms of today. It was all very confusing.

"The church offered no other option, and of course there were big, famous ministries pushing gay kids to change—it was awful. None of that worked and Derek just got more and more depressed. I'd been doing research and realized that most gay kids never had their sexual attraction changed, no matter how hard they tried. Of course, that's all understood now, at least by therapists and most of the rest of the world—certainly by your generation. I'm afraid the church is slow on this one and will end up on the wrong side of history."

Amy felt so relieved to meet someone who understood what she was going through. It was like getting a drink of water after a hike in the Nevada desert. "You're right! I've had gay friends since middle school. I can't believe God would love them any less. Did you leave the church?"

"My husband and I finally realized that we were going to lose our son. We went to our pastor with some of the research and the different scriptural interpretations we'd found and he flat out told us we were in sin. We had to choose, and we chose our son. We told him we loved him just the way he was and trusted God for his life. We left that church and eventually I went to seminary and became the pastor in a more affirming church denomination. The whole thing has left its mark on Derek, I'm afraid. He hasn't been back to church but he's married now and his husband, Drew, is a love. They come over for dinner a lot and we are thrilled to have them. We hope that someday he'll come back around."

"That's amazing," said Amy. "It makes me so mad at the church, though."

"Oh, I was livid! And my husband—he almost lost his faith over it. It took a few years. But what we've found is that God is so much bigger than we ever imagined. We started a ministry; it's a small group, really, to bridge the gap between those from the LGBTQI community who had been hurt by the church, and faith. We call it Shalom."

"Shalom?"

"Yes, it means more than just peace. It also means unity, completion, and fulfillment. We believe the body of Christ isn't complete until everyone is welcome at the table."

"Oh, Celeste." Amy grabbed the older woman's hand. "You can't imagine how it helps to hear that. I wish there was something like Shalom in Reno."

"Well, maybe you should start something."

Amy sat back in her chair, stunned. "Wow—maybe I should." Her mind raced with the possibilities. Joshua could help her; they could find others who'd been kicked out of churches or hurt in them. She definitely wanted to talk to Joshua, but there was no time now. The optional session was about grief, and she really wanted to know what Tom and Felicia had to say about that. She said good-bye and thank you to Celeste, who was opting for a nap. She hugged the woman tightly and headed to the meeting room. On the way to the meeting room, she saw Amani sitting by a window, reading. She felt the urge to go check on her but resisted. *If she needs help, she'll ask somebody,* she coached herself.

The room looked different than she'd seen it before. The lights were off and the only illumination was from candles. The large group of chairs was now a smaller group of chairs, and there was quiet music playing in the background. She took a seat and let her eyes adjust to the darkness. Tom and Felicia sat at the head of the circle, and in the center was a beautiful display of mugs and candles on a multitiered table. As Amy's eyes adjusted to the light, she could see that the cups were broken in different ways, some smashed, some only lightly chipped, some missing handles. She was very curious now. She could see Natalie across from her and they shared a small wave.

Once people stopped coming in, Felicia began. "We're glad you came. Grief is an unexpected consequence of working with people on the margins, and unless we acknowledge it and allow God to heal it, we become wounded wounders instead of wounded healers. Some of us have been hurt by the things we've seen and the evil we've encountered as we've served the poor. Some of us have been wounded by colleagues we've worked with, those we've served, or the churches that have sent us. Grief comes from a loss. But it doesn't have to be a death; it can be the loss of a job, a position, a friendship, a marriage."

Images of the losses she'd experienced flashed through Amy's mind like a slide show. Was that her problem? She'd never really allowed herself to grieve?

"This exercise is between you and the Divine," said Tom. "In a moment, we'll release you to choose a mug. Or, let the mug choose you. Then, we want you to take the mug off to study, to pray into. Let God speak to you through the mug about your brokenness and grief. Come back by one forty-five and, if you are ready, lay your mug at the foot of the cross. If not you can keep it until you are." He gestured to a cross standing against the far wall and illuminated by candles. Amy hadn't even noticed it. "Once you've released your mug, return to your seats. If you aren't ready to release your mug, you may keep it to pray into until you are. It's between you and God, but you can still join us back here for the closing ceremony. Now you may see which mug calls out to you."

Some people jumped up immediately, as if they'd been hearing mugs scream at them. Natalie was one of them. She grabbed a mug that had a huge chip out of it and left the room. Amy waited until the initial group had cleared until she pondered the mugs. She looked at one with a significant crack down its side but then her eyes landed on a mug that looked like a Monet painting. Its handle was broken off, and she grabbed it. She loved Monet. The peaceful pastels of his paintings had always calmed her soul. Mug in hand, she decided to go down to her room for the reflection—she'd need her journal for this one.

Once there, she realized that she really needed to clean her room. It was a mess. Clothes blanketed every surface; the sink was littered with makeup and hair supplies. It felt depressing. But with a sad smile she realized that it reflected her inner life pretty well: she was a mess. Tomorrow was their Sabbath. Tomorrow they had the whole day off. She'd clean it then.

She pulled up the covers on her bed and propped her pillow against the backrest. Grabbing the pillow off the extra bed, she added it to the pile and then opened the blinds to let in the afternoon light. Outside her window were shades of green—trees, grass, and bushes all looking inviting. She should have gone outside.

But the cup on her nightstand was calling to her, so she kicked off her shoes and sat on her bed, adjusting her pillows for support. She took the mug and inspected it. It had a white background with a print of Monet's water lilies. It was beautiful and perfect, except for the handle that was broken off. Two stubs stuck out from the mug's side where the handle had been.

Amy felt the mug: it was cool and clean with a glazed surface. The nubs of the missing handle were rough in contrast. Amy sat the mug on her lap and picked up her journal and pen. "Okay, I'm listening. What do you want to say to me?"

To her surprise, what came to her mind was not all the pain she had recently shared with Celeste. What came to her mind was . . . Thailand.

13

That night at their triad, Amy jumped in. "I'd like to share my story tonight if that's okay."

Hasmita and Connie nodded. Stephen leaned in to listen. Amy took a breath and began. "This conference is so intense!"

"Tell me about it," agreed Connie. "I'm exhausted. I'm so glad we have tomorrow off."

Hasmita smiled. "Don't tell anyone, but I've been taking many of the sessions off. I just can't take it all in. I've been joining those women who brought the adult coloring books," she giggled. "It's really relaxing."

Amy smiled; she felt glad about that. She'd seen the girls coloring during breaks. Amani was among them. It was probably hard to contextualize all of this as a Muslim or a Hindu. She was glad they were finding a way to support each other. Especially since she'd been fighting her desire to be "helpful" when no one was asking for help.

"I slept all afternoon," said Stephen. "Just needed a break; plus, I couldn't sleep last night—too much to think about." He looked like he was suppressing a grin when he glanced at Amy.

She felt blood rush to her face when she remembered the scene from last night. Was that just last night? She exhaled. "Well, I went to the grief workshop. I saw you there, Connie." She smiled at the woman with dark circles under her eyes. "They had us pick a mug that was broken. Some were smashed, some chipped, some cracked. Then we had to journal about our grief and losses as we looked at the mug." Amy gazed around at the circle of faces, each listening attentively to her. She nodded as if willing the words from her mouth. "So, I'm just going to tell you." They waited; no one spoke.

"After college I went on this thing called the Race for Missions. It was this mission trip that went to a different country for a month, twelve countries in a year. It was amazing. We were exposed to incredible work all over the world, people that worked with boy soldiers in Africa, an orphanage in Romania, an abandoned baby rescue in Korea . . ."

"Whoa," Stephen said. "That does sound amazing."

"It was," agreed Amy. "But I was most drawn to the work in Thailand. It was a sex trafficking rescue. So, after the Race for Missions, I decided to go back there and work with that organization. We hung out in the bars with the girls that were trapped in prostitution. Some had been sold into slavery by their families when they were only children. Some had been lured to the city by people promising jobs and then tricked into sex slavery. It was awful."

Hasmita shook her head. "I've heard this from some of the immigrants I work with. Some have been brought here as slaves in the workforce. No one knows they are here and they are kept working long hours with the promise of freedom and pay but not ever let go. It's horrible."

"Yes," said Amy. "But I loved working with the girls. We'd hang out and talk to them; then eventually we'd invite them to our home and introduce them to our job-training center. We trained them in sewing and English as a way to help them get out of the sex trade. We saw several become free through those years. But the problem for me was a woman named Anong. Her name means "beautiful woman," and she was beautiful, inside and out. I met her almost the first day I was there and it took a year and a half to get her out of the bars. She was in our training program and doing really well. I felt so proud of her because it was a really hard choice for her to leave the bars. She could make so much more by selling herself, and was getting a lot of pressure from her family to send money.

"One day we were walking around the market together when a private taxi pulled up next to us. She turned to me and . . ." Amy felt tears rush to her eyes at the crystal-clear memory. She smelled the spicy smells of the Thai market, heard the loud cacophony of traffic rushing by, saw entire families on one scooter, women in colorful clothes, ragged children running around. It was all right there, so fresh to all of her senses. She steadied herself. "Anong turned to me, and with tears in her eyes she said, "I'm sorry, Amy." A door opened on the taxi next to her and she got in. I could see a white, middle-aged man in a business suit on the seat next to her. The car drove off, and I can still see her face pressed against the window, tears in her eyes."

Amy took a few calming breaths to ground herself fully back in the present. Connie reached over and squeezed her hand.

"Where did she go?" asked Hasmita.

"I found out later from one of the bar girls that she'd gone off with an American for his monthlong business trip. She couldn't say no to the money. She'd told me about him before . . . He liked to beat her." Amy shook her head at the memory as a tear slid down her cheek.

"American?" asked Stephen.

"Yeah," said Amy, hearing the disgust in her own voice. "Thais buying Thais is the biggest problem. A lot of men there have what they call 'little wives' on the side. But Westerners make up a large chunk of the customers too. Sixty-six percent of men that land in Bangkok for 'business' are actually there for sex tourism."

"Ugh," said Stephen, looking like he might be sick. "That makes me want to hurt someone."

Amy appreciated the sentiment. She'd felt it so many days herself.

"Anyway, I never heard from Anong again. And I now realize that as a two on the Enneagram, who likes to help people, I took her defection very personally. Shortly after that I got sick. Really sick. The organization decided it was best if I came back to the States to recuperate. My home church, who had been my biggest supporters, decided that I couldn't go back overseas without the covering of an actual missions organization."

"Wait," said Hasmita. "I don't understand. Please explain this to me."

"Sorry," said Amy, realizing that she'd slipped into Christianese and needed to be more careful. Hasmita probably had no context for some of those terms. "I was working for an organization in Thailand, but I had no sending organization from America. I was like a free agent, working overseas. There are organizations here that send . . . justice workers and look out for their welfare and make sure they are okay. My church wanted me to go back, but only if I went back under the care of one of those agencies, instead of just going on my own like I did. I had found the organization in Thailand on my Race for Missions and just gone to Thailand to join in their work, with no U.S. protection."

"Oh, I see," said Hasmita. "Thank you."

"I know it's probably not what you want to hear," said Stephen, "but I think that sounds wise."

"Yeah," agreed Amy. "I was kind of butthurt at first, but I understood. I mean, they were looking out for me, right?"

Stephen nodded.

"But that begins the second part of my story."

"Oh my," said Connie.

"Yeah, it kind of sucks," said Amy. "My home church is amazing. It's one of those megachurch types and I grew up in it and always loved it. When I got home, and was healing, I got involved in different activities with the church. My best friend, Joshua, was the youth leader, so I helped him with skits and I set up an interactive prayer room—stuff like that. I met this guy named West who was new to the church. We hit it off right away and things were great.

"Then when our outreach director resigned, someone suggested that I should apply for the job. It seemed perfect for me, and I wasn't really ready to go back overseas. I was still hurting, I guess."

"What is an outreach director?" asked Hasmita.

"Good question," said Amy, trying to remember to slow down. "The job covered the overseas and local outreaches of the church. My job was to keep track of all the people the church supported, as well as find ways to keep their ministries in front of the congregation. It was perfect for me and even though I knew I was young, I decided to apply, and I got the job!"

"Sounds like a good fit," said Stephen.

"It was," Amy said wistfully. She really loved that job. "I was only in it for about six months when the problem started."

"Oh, here we go," said Connie, her forehead wrinkled. If anyone understood church politics, it was Connie.

Amy smiled at her gratefully. "Okay, this part might be kind of controversial. But . . . it's my story, so I'm going to tell it."

"Yes," encouraged Hasmita. "Be honest. This is a safe place."

"Thank you," said Amy. "My best friend, Joshua—remember he was the youth leader? Well, he's gay. And I always knew that, and it was never an issue. Our church was a welcoming place—at least that's what they said. We had gay people in our congregation, even couples. But I guess I never realized that it was a conditional acceptance. When Joshua fell in love . . . with a boy . . ."

"The shit hit the fan," said Stephen. "Oops, excuse my French."

That made Amy smile, especially since he'd heard her shouting profanities from the orchard.

"Yep, exactly," she said. "The 'powers that be' called him out on it, but Joshua wouldn't back down. They fired him." Amy's heart broke all over again thinking of Joshua's face when he came to tell her the news. Grief etched lines on his beautiful face; his heart was broken.

"That's awful," said Connie, "but typical."

Stephen nodded and Hasmita smiled gently. She may not understand, thought Amy, but she still cares about me. She took courage and went on. "I was pretty upset and went to my pastor, saying, 'Surely this is a mistake, right? I mean, Joshua has been in this church since he was born. Everyone loves him. He's the best youth group leader we've ever had and you're firing him?'" Amy's voice grew in volume and disbelief as she spoke, remembering how stunned she had felt when the pastor sat before her, unmoved by her tears.

"Bet that didn't go so well," said Stephen.

"You got that right," said Amy with heat in her voice. "He basically said I had a choice to make. The church had decided to release a statement saying that they believed in marriage between one man and one woman and I was being asked to choose to agree with it or leave." Amy's heartbeat quickened at the memory.

"Did they give you time to decide?" asked Hasmita.

"Two weeks!" said Amy. "I had to meet with the elder board in two weeks with my answer. My dad is an elder! I was devastated. This wasn't a primary doctrinal issue—I mean, no one was going to meet Jesus in heaven and have to answer 'How do you feel about gays?' to get in."

Stephen laughed at that. "True."

"I just don't understand why the church has drawn this particular line in the sand. Didn't Jesus model caring for the marginalized? He would be the first to love Joshua unconditionally, and now Christians, his own church family, were kicking him to the curb."

"It's a very polarizing issue for some reason," agreed Connie.

"I think it's fear," said Stephen. "People fear what they don't understand. Like racial prejudice or how women have been treated in the church. Change is hard for people; they like the status quo. White people fear blacks because they don't know any. The same is true of people from the LGBTQI community. If you don't know anyone from it, or at least think you don't, it's easy to vilify them."

"Exactly!" said Amy.

"So what happened?" asked Hasmita.

Amy slumped back in her chair. "I went to the elder board and said all of those things. And they asked me to 'tender my resignation.' Like it was my idea to leave or something!"

"Ouch," said Connie. "Was your dad at that meeting?"

"No," breathed Amy. She'd been glad about that. "He recused himself—but after he said he understood where they were coming from!"

"It's like when I left my husband," said Connie. "Suddenly your whole church family turns against you."

"Yes!" said Amy. "Like all your years of faithfulness count for nothing. Suddenly, you're suspect. All the respect you've earned goes out the window. West quickly dumped me too." She looked at the floor, face hot. That still stung.

"Good riddance," said Connie. "If he was that shallow, you should be glad to be rid of him."

"Someone once told me," said Stephen, his voice soft, "that churches are three things: a fellowship, a family, and an organization. So if you get fired by the organization, you also get fired by your family and your fellowship. You lose all three at once."

Amy felt her throat constrict. That was exactly what had happened to her, and to Joshua. She'd lost more than just a job; she'd lost her whole faith community. She nodded, unable to speak.

"Let's hold Amy's story," said Stephen. "That is a lot of pain for one person to carry."

They bowed their heads and Amy felt loved and supported in the silence that followed. She felt something else too. She felt lighter, as if sharing the burden made it less heavy to bear.

14

Amy woke up happy on Wednesday. Happy because it was their Sabbath, a day of silence, solitude, and rest. In fact, she had slept straight through breakfast and woke up just in time for lunch. At breakfast and lunch, they were required to sit in the silent cafeteria area, but at dinner, they had the option of sitting in the regular room if they wanted to talk over their meal.

Amy was happy to sit in silence at lunch. She took her time, sipped her coffee and relished her food. It was a little awkward to be sitting in a room full of people and not talking. She thought of Tom's instructions the day before. He said that God had given the Sabbath for a reason: "We all need a day to reboot our souls. To stop working and focus on rest and soul-filling activities like journaling, being out in nature, spending time in holy books or prayer."

The silence meant they weren't even supposed to make eye contact with each other. He called it Great Silence. That part felt a little weird to Amy; still, she was more than ready to have some time alone with her thoughts.

After lunch, she took a long shower. She was even going to give herself a day off from exercise! Not that Felicia was leading yoga today—she wasn't—but she could have gone for a run or a long walk. Maybe later—if she felt like it. Wow, having a day off with no agenda felt like freedom.

First, to tackle her room. Tom had said that the Buddhists have a saying: "Before enlightenment, chop wood, carry water. After enlightenment, chop wood, carry water." She thought maybe it

meant that the small things, like cleaning her room, were important to the state of her soul.

It only took about a half hour to get her room clean and her
bed made. She curled up in the chair by the window and surveyed
her work. Yes, it was more peaceful this way. She grabbed her
journal and turned to her list, adding, "Nine: clean my room once
a week." Then, because she'd been thinking about it, she added,
"Ten: practice the examen daily." And because this day of rest felt
so freeing, she quickly added, "Eleven: take a weekly Sabbath." She
didn't know how exactly she would accomplish that with school
and needing to find a job, but she'd sure try.

After journaling for an hour, Amy was feeling stiff. She
decided it was time to explore. She'd still never been in the chapel
where they did the examen in the daytime. She walked through
the center, seeing people here and there enjoying their own Sabbath. Even inside the chapel she was not alone. Three others were
spread out on the wooden chairs. Two sat with their eyes closed;
one was writing.

She slid into a seat away from the others. The room was large
and not what she'd expected. She thought there would be more
ornamentation, but the room was fairly stark, wooden chairs with
blue-padded seats in a horseshoe around a simple wooden altar.
The walls were constructed in bowed cement squares that held what
looked like speakers or organ piping. The high ceilings were open
to wooden beams holding up lights. She did find it beautiful in its
simplicity. Perhaps the place needed no adornment. It was just a
God space and there was plenty of room. Is that why she suddenly
wanted to keep her own room uncluttered? To create more space
for God? It was time to toss things out, get rid of some things both
material and emotional. She sat in the room and prayed until her
bum got sore. Then it was time to take a walk outside.

It was a perfect day for pondering, kind of overcast and muggy.
It felt good to be outside and moving her body. She walked the lake,

trying the breathing exercises she'd learned. What did she want to do with the rest of her Sabbath? She remembered that Tom said they could pray with the monks, and headed back to her room.

On the desk sat the information booklet she'd seen but pushed aside the first day. Inside was some information about the center and a schedule of when the monks prayed. The next prayer time was six o'clock. That was right after dinner. Thinking of it, her stomach growled. She was feeling kind of antsy—a whole day in silence felt like a lot. She wondered if she'd ever been quiet for a whole day before, or even a whole hour without using her technology. She decided to read until dinner, then go to the regular dining room so she could talk to someone, then to Vespers where the monks prayed.

Having a plan helped her settle down, and she enjoyed reading, then walked hurriedly down to the dining room as soon as it opened.

The few people in the room were gathering around one table. Amy joined them gladly with her tray of food. She sat down next to an African American woman who was not involved in conversation and introduced herself. "I'm Christine," the woman said in return, "and welcome to the table of extroverts!" Amy laughed, excited to be among the speaking, at least for a while.

Christine was really nice, a professor at a historically black college, though she looked too young for that to Amy. "How has this week been for you so far?" Amy asked.

Christine looked thoughtful. "For me, personally, it's been good. But I'm trying to figure out how to take the things I'm learning back to my people. These forms of prayer are not easy to translate to my context. We are not known for being particularly quiet."

Amy laughed. "I never thought about how white these forms of prayer are."

"Even with their Eastern roots," said Christine, "they feel very European. But I'm learning so much and it's been really good for me. Still . . . I'll have to think of some ways to make it more accessible."

Amy nodded. Probably any person of color at this retreat would have to do that. She wasn't sure how to ask what she was wondering. "Has it been . . . hard being here? Because . . . it's mostly white?"

Christine looked at her with what appeared to be interest. "Well, yes it has, and thank you for asking. But to be honest, outside of my college, this kind of displacement is my life."

"Displacement?"

"Displacement is being the only person like you in any environment. Like me being here, or at the store or a job anywhere in Nebraska."

"That would probably be true in Reno, where I live, too."

Christine focused on Amy with eyes that held a challenge. "Amy, have you ever displaced yourself?"

Amy considered the question. Then smiled. "I have! I lived overseas for several years. I didn't know the language, the customs, the food. Yep, I definitely did."

"That's fantastic!" said Christine and took a sip of her water. "Displacement is a huge part of understanding what it is like to be a minority in a majority culture."

"Man, I bet your students love you!"

A man in a black robe stepped up to the table. "May I join you?" It was the monk who had welcomed them to the center. His German accent made Amy's heart warm.

"Please do," she said.

"I'm Father Paul," he said.

Amy and Christine introduced themselves. He had kind eyes, a short gray beard, and salt-and-pepper hair. "Are you ladies enjoying your time here?"

"Oh yes," said Amy, and Christine nodded, her mouth full of salad. "We were just talking about how much we've learned. I was wondering about the Benedictines. Can you tell us more? I don't know anything, except what I've read in the brochure."

"Me either," agreed Christine.

"Of course," said Father Paul, spreading butter on his bread. "Each Benedictine monastery is slightly different because each one is autonomous, but we follow a basic rule for life, integrating prayer, manual labor, and study into a balanced existence. This monastery's mission is to provide the hospitality of this retreat center as a spiritual oasis in the desert of life, but we also do a lot with missions, especially in Africa." He took a bite of his bread.

Amy had noticed a whole room of African artifacts during her wandering that morning. "It's certainly been an oasis for me!" said Amy.

"For me as well," agreed Christine.

Father Paul chuckled. "I'm very glad to hear that. Have you had a chance to join us for prayer?"

"I've been coming to the morning prayers," said Christine.

Amy was impressed. Those were at 6:35 in the morning.

"Except today. Today I slept in."

Father Paul chuckled again. "As you should on your retreat Sabbath. How about you, Amy?"

Surprised he remembered her name, Amy felt glad she had a positive answer. "I'm planning to come tonight, right after this."

"Very good," he said, smiling.

"My grandfather was from Germany," she added. "Wuppertal."

"Ah," he said, "not far from where I was born in Bonn! Have you ever been there?"

"Oh yes; I've been there twice. I loved it. And we traveled a bit, so I saw some of Bonn. We toured the beautiful old government buildings."

"Excuse me," said Christine. "I'm heading back into silence. It was great sharing dinner with you." She stood and took her tray as Amy waved and smiled, hoping they hadn't chased her way.

"Sprichst du Deutsch?" he asked.

"Sehr wenig," she replied, holding her fingers up to indicate she only spoke a little German.

"Ah, well," he smiled. "I get homesick sometimes."

"I bet," she said.

"Well, I must get ready for prayers. I will see you there?"

"Yes, I'll be there."

15

Amy followed other silent retreatants across the parking lot to the monastery chapel. She was curious to experience the Catholic service, since she'd never been in one. Maybe she'd missed her calling as a nun.

Inside was a room much smaller than the big chapel but similar in style, with wooden walls and pews, instead of chairs, in a horseshoe shape around a plain altar. Hanging from the open-beamed ceiling on cables was an African Jesus statue hanging on a cross.

Amy was guided into a pew and handed a book that looked like a hymnal and the monk that guided her whispered, "Please don't sing along with us," which Amy found odd.

She could tell there were people here from the community as well. At the front of the room a monk came forward to lead. The order of the service felt foreign to Amy, a displacement experience, she realized. She could not follow along very well with what was happening and was always surprised when people near her stood or knelt. The monks took turns singing, and she tried to keep up in the book. When it ended, she was glad she had come but still not entirely comfortable. So much for her calling as a nun.

At the end she managed to smile at Father Paul and head happily out the door. The air was warm, so she decided to go sit by the lake. She found a plastic chair facing the water and settled in. Closing her eyes, she felt the soft air touching her face. Something about the night made her feel sad. Was it the silence? No one to talk to but herself? She'd come to this retreat angry. Now she felt less angry but more sad. The things she'd always believed were now in a heap of things she might want to discard. How was she supposed to navigate this?

A tear slid down Amy's cheek. More than anything she wanted to talk to someone about it. She was so used to processing things with her friends. Now it was just her and . . . God. *Do you still speak to me, God?* she wondered in the direction of the stars. *Do you still like me? I don't like me much. I'm judgmental, bossy, and a people pleaser.*

Random thoughts flitted through her mind as she reviewed the week. It was like taking a jar of river water and letting the sediment settle to the bottom. The water became clearer as she sat. She could see herself more clearly too and wasn't loving the view.

After about an hour, she dragged herself back to the room. Maybe she'd just go to bed early. Maybe she was just tired. She got ready for bed then looked at the clock. She was surprised to see it was barely eight. Did she really want to go to bed this early?

She pulled out her journal and started writing.

Suddenly it was morning. What had woken Amy up? Her neck was sore from falling asleep in an awkward position. At some point, she must have crawled under her covers. Her phone buzzed, a text from Josh.

JOSH: Call me!

It must have been the phone that had woken her. She quickly pulled on her yoga gear and, rubbing sleep from her eyes, she dashed down the hall and out of the building. The morning sun was just coming up and the sky was a brilliant pink. The air was cool and moist against her skin. It was six o'clock in the morning, which made it four in the morning for Josh. Was he okay? Quickly she walked to the one spot on the grounds she'd found the best signal, across from and to the right of the statue. How had his text gotten through? She pressed his name on her favorites, hoping for a good signal.

"Amy!" said his happy voice.

"Are you okay? It's the middle of the night."

"I know but I'm so happy I couldn't sleep and waited as long as I could to call you—Peter proposed to me! I'm getting married!"

Amy rocked back on her heels. Married? Joshua was getting married? Part of her was delighted—he was so happy. Part of her was concerned. Marriage equality had just come to Nevada, but it still was not a great place to be gay. And part of her was jealous. *Even my gay friends get married before I do!* "Tigger, that's fantastic! Tell me everything."

He spoke in a rush. "Well, we'd gone to the movies—you know, the one downtown—and after, he said he wanted to walk around. So, we were just strolling around. It was warm and beautiful out, and I'm totally clueless, and he takes me to the bridge on Virginia Street—you know, the one they rebuilt? The one you threw your ring off of? And we're leaning over the edge and he says, 'This is the bridge the people who came to Reno in the fifties, to get those quick divorces, used to throw their rings off of.'"

"What?" said Amy, getting caught up in the excitement of his story.

"I know, right? Then he bends down, like he's going to tie his shoe, and says, 'Oh my God, look! I found one!'"

"And I look down and he's kneeling on one knee with a wedding ring in a box!"

"No way! Oh my gosh—he didn't! That is awesome!"

"I know, right? It was crazy. But Amy, I'm so excited. And we want to get married next summer, and I want you to be my best man." Amy could practically see his smile on the other end of the line. She laughed. It felt so good to share his joy.

"Hmmm," she said. "Do I get to throw you a bachelor party?"

"Of course!"

They talked more, and finally Joshua was tired enough to sleep. Amy was enjoying the morning and decided to walk around the lake. "Early phone call?" asked Stephen, who'd jogged up from the opposite direction and turned to walk with her. He was wearing his 49ers shirt and sweating.

"You've been out running already?"

"Yeah, I like to run—it clears my head. You look happy. Good news?"

She smiled. "My best friend, Joshua, got engaged last night! He asked me to be his best man." Then she bit her lip. "Don't know how you feel about all that."

"Oh, I was in my sister's gay wedding in May. You know, love conquers all." He smiled at her. "I really appreciated your story the other night. Thanks for sharing it. Sounds like you've been through a tough time."

"Thanks," said Amy. "I realized I completely forgot to tell you guys about the cups! That was how the story started."

"Well," he said, smiling, "tell me now."

Amy wished he wasn't so good-looking. His wedding band flashed in the sunlight. She suddenly became aware that she had run out of her room without even brushing her teeth. Did she have morning breath? She turned slightly away from him as she spoke. "I took this broken mug to my room. It had Monet's water lilies on it, with a broken-off handle. And I sort of saw how it was like me." He nodded and she went on as they passed the statue of St. Benedict, hands reaching over the lake. "As I looked at the broken handle, I felt like the things I held onto are gone: my church, my idea about missions, my potential marriage, my identity as a Christian—at least as an evangelical Christian. But then it was like God said, 'The cup is still beautiful and useful. It's not broken beyond repair.' And I realized that my life is still beautiful and useful, and I've realized this week that my faith is not broken beyond repair."

"Wow! All that from a cup? Wish I'd gone to that session. What do you do now—since the church blowout?"

"I'm in grad school—social work."

"Oh, that's right. You said that the first night."

"I'm supposed to be finishing. I need to start writing my thesis, but I'm not sure what I want to do it on."

"I've got a couple of observations, if you're open to hear them." He smiled and she noticed he had a dimple on his left cheek but not one on his right. She quickly glanced away.

"Sure."

"Two things come to mind. One, you seem to have a heart for the LGBTQI population—you could do something on that."

"That's funny! Someone else mentioned that."

"And . . . are you still interested in working with trafficked people?"

"Yeah, I guess I am."

"Are there any trafficked people in Reno?"

Her mind whirled at the thought. "That's a really good question." Was anyone working with trafficked victims in Reno? "Prostitution is legal there. Oh my gosh—I've lived there my whole life and never thought about that before. I need to find out what's going on in the area with trafficked kids. Wow Stephen! You've just given me the best idea for research I'd actually enjoy!"

They had finished the lap around the little lake and were back at the entrance to the retreat center. Stephen pointed across at St. Benedict. "I always think he looks like he's doing an end-zone dance."

Amy laughed. "Are you kidding? I thought the same thing the first time I saw him! I called him Benny and decided he was a 49er."

Stephen held open the door for her. "My kinda girl! You should come down sometime for a game. I have season tickets."

Amy smiled as she passed through the door. "That'd be great."
You, me, and the wife, she thought, unsure what to think of the
invitation. People inside were in the breakfast line. They joined
the end of it and the guy with the hipster beard started ribbing
Stephen about his 49ers T-shirt.

Amy's mind was full of ideas and quickly tuned out their foot-
ball banter. Reno, sex trafficking. It was a natural—why hadn't
she thought of it before? Natalie and Brooke waved at her, gesturing that they should eat together. She nodded, glad for a chance
to connect with her friends. She said good-bye to Stephen and
moved up the line to join them. She had so much to tell.

16

"I can't believe this is our last full day," said Natalie over breakfast. "In the middle, it felt like it would never end, and now . . ."

"Seriously," Brooke broke in, "this has been off the hook. We need to keep in touch."

"Yes!" said Natalie. "I have so much to process."

At that all three girls pulled out their phones, laughed, and started sharing their information to each other.

Natalie's giant doe eyes got bigger as she leaned in conspiratorially. "You guys think we could maybe . . . meet here again next year?"

Brooke jumped in. "Or maybe find another event somewhere else like it to attend!"

"That would be amazing!" said Amy.

"Let's all look at our faves and send each other ideas," gushed Natalie. "I'd love to see Brené Brown or Elizabeth Gilbert."

"Or Sarah Bessey or Nadia Bolz-Weber," added Brooke.

"Or Rachel Held Evans or Anne Lamott," said Amy. She didn't know some of the names but thought anyone Natalie and Brooke were interested in would be fun to see.

"Time for yoga," said Natalie, getting up from the table and gathering their dishes.

"You guys wanna meet in the parking lot tonight after the examen?" asked Brooke.

"One last time," said Natalie. "I'm in."

"Me too," said Amy, glad she'd have one more chance to visit with her friends before they all took off for home in the morning.

She stacked her tray on the racks for dirty dishes and followed her friends to yoga.

In the morning session, the seats were in rows again. After the breath prayers, Tom put a picture up on the screen. It was an odd picture to Amy. It looked like three people sitting at a table. It was not a pretty picture. It was definitely something religious, like the art she saw in the hallways of this building.

"Today we are going to talk about reading icons."

Amy remembered Celeste had said something about icons. What was it?

Tom began clicking through a PowerPoint full of names, dates, and pictures as he spoke. "Images of Christ and the apostles were painted right away after Christ's death, but soon church leaders said it was wrong to have images because people could worship them instead of Christ. When Constantine made Christianity the state religion, icons were allowed and iconographers thrived into the eighth and ninth centuries. Icons were called 'windows to the divine' or 'windows to heaven.' They were not drawn; they were referred to as 'written,' and they were meant to be read. The method of writing them was passed down through the centuries and involved a lot of prayer; they were made to teach the liturgy, to teach theology, and to open a window into the very presence of God.

"Unfortunately, they fell out of favor once again during the Reformation. The Protestants thought there should be no images adorning churches. Today, most icons can be found in Eastern Orthodox churches, although you can see some around here if you look closely. But Protestants are rediscovering the joy of praying an icon, and we're going to try it today."

Praying an icon, thought Amy. She'd never heard of that. How had she missed out on so much? The screen once again held the original picture of the three people at the table.

"The first thing you should know," said Tom, "is that icons are written in inverse perspective. It's the opposite of the perspective we are used to seeing where the vanishing point is deep in the painting. With inverse perspective, the vanishing point is back behind you, inviting you into the painting."

Amy had taken an art class and understood about vanishing points. Her eye was used to looking into the painting, with the far-off things small and the near things bigger. She wondered if it was the inverse perspective that made these pictures look ugly to her.

"This," said Tom, gesturing to the picture, "is Rublev's icon of the Trinity. This is both the story of the three angels that appeared to and ate with Abraham at the Oak of Mamre and a picture of the Father, Son, and Holy Spirit inviting you to sit with them."

Wow, I never would have seen all that, thought Amy, noticing that the figures were indeed angels with golden wings behind them and halos over their heads. She wondered if the original audience would have been able to see all this without an interpreter.

"See the tree behind them—the Oak of Mamre—the house of Abraham, and the mountain in the background. Notice the color of their robes. The Son, in the middle, is wearing the red-brown robe with a blue cloak. He represents the divine in heaven and earth. His hand points toward the Spirit on our right. The Father sends the Son; the Son sends the Spirit. He is both human and divine, touching the earth and blessing the chalice on the table. His head is inclined to the left, toward his Father. The Father, in the golden robe, represents heaven. He has his hand up in blessing toward the Son. The Spirit wears pale blue and fragile green, moving among both the earth and sky. All three figures hold a staff of authority."

Amy squinted at the screen. She had not noticed the thin lines of a staff next to each figure. This was interesting.

"And the Spirit gestures to an opening at the table, an invitation to the empty place, where you are invited to join them. See how their heads each incline to the other in a circle of love and fellowship. That is where you are being invited in, to the hospitality of the Trinity."

Whoa. For some reason, that felt scary to Amy—the idea to pull up to the table with the three parts of the Trinity.

"What I'd like you to try as you gaze at this icon is allow yourself to sit at the table with them. Interact with each part of the Trinity. See which part you feel most comfortable with, which is most uncomfortable to you. We'll do this for the remainder of the hour. Perhaps talk to them about your feelings."

Amy looked at the painting and tried to put herself at the table. She closed her eyes to picture it. She gazed at the Father, and all her old Sunday school images came back: long white beard, white robe. Her mental image of Jesus was pretty Sunday school–ish too: the white—despite being Middle Eastern—guy with the brown beard who was usually portrayed holding a lamb or a child on his lap. The Holy Spirit was harder to picture, and she was reminded of a book she'd read called *The Shack,* where God was portrayed as a black woman and the Holy Spirit as an Asian woman. Was it the fact that they were portrayed as women that made them both seem much more accessible to her?

Closing her eyes was not working. She gazed at the picture and quieted her mind and pictured herself at the table. Feeling what it would be like to sit with the Father. Good. She felt comfortable there; her image of God was good and loving. She let herself reach over to Jesus. That felt good too, safe. Jesus had been her friend since she was small. But when she faced the Holy Spirit, she felt uneasy. *I guess I don't know who you are,* she said in her mind. *My church never mentioned you much. Maybe I need to try to get to know you better,* she concluded. And she felt as if the fuzzy figure replied, "I'd like that."

Amy made sure to sit with Celeste at lunch. They exchanged contact information too. And Celeste had shared her joy over Joshua's announcement and Amy's description of praying the icon.

"What do you think you'll take home with you from here, Amy?"

Amy had to think about that as she picked at her salad. "I feel like I'll need more time to process. I've met such amazing people and learned so many things. But . . . one thing is . . . I feel like God hasn't given up on me and I haven't given up on him. Our relationship has changed, but that's not necessarily a bad thing."

"Actually, I think it's a very good thing. Worth the price of admission, if you ask me!"

Amy smiled at that. She would miss Celeste. "Do you ever meet with people—you know, long distance? Like maybe on Skype or something?"

Celeste smiled. "As a spiritual director, I do."

"What is a spiritual director exactly?"

"A spiritual director is someone trained to sit with someone and companion their spiritual journey. Generally, we'd talk monthly for an hour, over Skype, but it's more about listening to God together."

"Oh my gosh!" said Amy. "Would you be willing to do that for me?"

Celeste laughed. "I have to tell you that spiritual direction generally costs a little money. I usually charge forty dollars a session and I'd feel weird bringing money into our friendship."

"No way," said Amy. "It would be so worth it to get some direction spiritually. You've already helped me so much. But . . . I don't exactly have a job."

"How about this," said Celeste. "We'll start meeting monthly from now until you get your next job. Then we'll see what you can afford. Would that work out for you?"

"Would it ever! Thank you so much!" Hope surged through Amy like fire. She wouldn't be alone in this journey. There were her new friends and Celeste to guide her and keep her moving forward.

"Are you going to the special session after lunch?" asked Celeste.

"Yes; are you?"

"No, I'm giving myself a break to pack. I have to leave very early and I tend to poop out right after the examen. I might take a nap if I get packed up quick enough. But I'm glad you're going. SoulCollage is one of my favorite spiritual exercises."

"Wow, we've learned so many," said Amy. "I definitely want to keep trying Lectio and the examen. Today I was even able to rest during the centering prayer, though I doubt I'll be trying that on my own yet. It did help, though, when Tom said the goal was to 'rest in the love of God.'"

"That helped me too! And when Felicia added that we are to 'ever so gently' bring ourselves back to our sacred word or picture. I think I was trying to swat the thoughts away like flies."

Amy giggled. "I think I was karate chopping them!"

"Well, you'd better run along to the session."

Amy started gathering up her dishes. "I'm so glad I don't have to really say good-bye to you, Celeste."

"I'm glad too, Amy."

Amy remembered how she'd almost missed meeting Celeste because of her sandals. *What a jerk,* she chided herself. *Look what I almost missed out on because of my shallow, judgmental attitude.* She mentally added a number to her thirty-things-to-do list: *Twelve: meet with a spiritual director. I need one,* she thought, nodding.

17

Amy walked into the main meeting room. The lights were low and a smaller circle of chairs had been set up on the left side of the room where Tom and Felicia were already seated. The other half of the room was full of tables. Some were heaped with papers and others looked bare except for scissors and glue. The session was entitled "Healing of the Trauma Brain," and Amy, who had signed up for pretty much everything, wasn't sure what the title referred to or what Celeste had meant by SoulCollage.

When the circle was full, Felicia nodded. "Unfortunately, being an activist exposes us to trauma. Not always directly, but even being exposed to secondhand trauma daily can give us some of the same symptoms as those who were directly exposed, especially when the people are as loving and caring as you all."

Amy wondered if she had been exposed to trauma. Seeing and hearing what the bar girls had been through was certainly traumatic, but had it affected her?

Tom held up his phone. "I'm going to time you for one minute and I just want you to breathe normally and count your breaths." He looked at his phone. "Ready, go."

Amy started counting. By the time Tom said, "Time," she'd counted eighteen.

"Now, what kind of numbers did you get?" asked Tom. Amy was surprised to hear the variety of numbers: twelve, eight, eighteen. What was the point and why were the numbers so variable?

Tom explained, "When we are in trauma, it actually changes the structure of our brains. Trauma brain is putting us in our lower, more animalistic brains where we are hypervigilant for attack." His hand swept the base of his skull. "We live in the 'fight, flight, or freeze' zone and our breathing becomes shallow and rapid in order to prepare us for survival."

Shock filled Amy. She'd had eighteen breaths in a minute, the largest number she'd heard. Was she living in constant fear?

Felicia said, "The good news is that our brains can be rewired. Trauma can be healed and we can function once again in our higher brain, where our logic center lies." She touched her forehead as she spoke. "We can do this by learning to breathe. That's why we have been starting each morning with a breathing exercise. It only takes three conscious gut breaths to balance our parasympathetic nervous system, and spiritual practices like the ones we've been teaching you can really help. Of course, if you're having nightmares and other debilitating stress symptoms, you should absolutely seek the help of a counselor who is familiar with post-traumatic stress disorder.

"PTSD is formed when three things happen at once. First, you are in a situation that feels safe and turns unsafe. Second, you are startled or surprised by something, and third, at some point, you feel like you might die." Felicia stopped, as if she knew they'd need time to absorb her last words.

"You can see why soldiers get PTSD," she said. "They are constantly in situations that turn dangerous, they get startled a lot, and they frequently feel that they might die."

Amy felt relieved to hear that. She wasn't having nightmares and no one was trying to kill her or anything—maybe she didn't have PTSD.

"So, let's start with some breathing exercises. You can basically Google 'breathing exercises' and find some that work for you. And there are a lot of great apps out there. We use one called the Insight Timer for centering prayer. It also comes with guided meditations."

Amy jotted down the name of the app and settled into her seat for the breathing exercises.

Tom began, "The goal is that your exhale would be longer than your inhale. Exhale through your pursed lips, like through a straw, to draw it out. This will help you slow down your breaths. Count the length of your inhales and exhales to see if you can make the length of your exhales longer than the length of your inhales. Let's do that for a few minutes."

Amy tried. She had a hard time getting her inhale past four beats and couldn't seem to get her exhale to last any longer. At the end of the exercise, she felt defeated.

"Don't worry if this is hard," said Felicia. "The key is to keep working at it. If you have a chance today, try walking around the lake. Take a step for each beat of your inhale and try to add an extra step to the exhale. It's part of retraining your brain and your lungs and takes time." They did two more breathing exercises. One that seemed beautiful, almost like a dance, which Felicia led them in, and one that Tom led that had them saying loud, silly syllables. She thought how funny they would look if a stranger walked in.

After all the breathing, they counted again, and Amy was surprised that she only took twelve breaths in a minute. It was working!

"Now," said Felicia, "we will be experiencing SoulCollage. Has anyone tried it before?"

Several people raised their hands. Amy noticed that none of her friends were in the session today, except Hasmita and Connie from her triad.

"Each of you will have a small piece of poster board," Felicia said, holding up an example the size of a half sheet of printer paper. "You'll walk around and look at the magazine pictures you find on the table and see what draws you. You might be drawn to a picture because it's beautiful, but you also might be drawn to a picture because it is ugly or disturbing to you in some way.

It's okay—just notice which ones draw you. When you find five or six pictures, go to one of the tables and arrange them to fit on the half page. You may need to trim them or let go of a picture at this point. There are scissors and glue at each table. Do this first; then we'll give more directions."

People slowly got up and headed to the tables. There were pictures spread out all over the tables, some whole pages, some ripped to just one photo. Extra *National Geographic* magazines were piled on a table.

Amy began to browse. She found a funny picture of a giraffe that looked like it had walked out of the trees and been startled by the photographer. It had a "deer in headlights" look to it. Then she found a beautiful flowered meadow, which she took, and there was this one of a bride in a ridiculously huge dress—it reminded her of the movie *My Big Fat Greek Wedding* with all the layers and bows. She passed it by and saw a picture that looked pretty but upon closer inspection was a bubbling swamp that looked like toxic waste. She wanted to pass it by but she was having a strong reaction to it and remembered what Felicia had said, so she grabbed it. A few more passes around the tables and she found a tunnel through a rock mountain that looked like it led somewhere beautiful and a piece of red-hot metal being forged on an anvil. The hands holding the hammer looked strong and she liked that. Then she took one more pass and the bride picture caught her eye again, so she grabbed it.

Hasmita and Connie were sitting together at a table, so she joined them. The room was quiet as everyone started trying to cut and paste their pictures to fit on the poster board. Amy found the activity rather relaxing. She was almost done when Felicia broke her concentration. "When you're finished, let yourself gaze at your picture and ponder this statement: 'I'm the one who . . .'"

Amy looked at her collage. From the upper left corner she saw the mucky swamp. The giraffe's head and torso seemed to float up from the swamp, looking surprised and confused. Her eyes followed down to the left where the metal was being shaped over the anvil; then the bride appeared. There wasn't room for much of her, so Amy had cut her down to just her torso, but her gaze was toward her beloved, who was out of the frame, and her hand rested lightly on his in a fun, flirty way. The last picture on the right was the tunnel through the rock. She'd put the flowered meadow across the whole page first, so wherever two pictures didn't meet, little flowers peeked through.

Amy studied the collage. "I'm the one who . . ." Then it came to her. She was the one who'd been dragged through the toxic mess at church. She was the giraffe: confused, startled, hurt. She'd thought things were safe, but they weren't—they'd turned hostile, and she'd been blindsided by the pain and betrayal.

Her eyes drifted left to the strong hands and the anvil-forged steel. She was being formed by the Father's hand. Then she saw the bride and her throat constricted. It was one of her favorite biblical images: God as bridegroom, she as bride. This brown-haired beauty sat in the white gown. She was a bride, looking to the left at her beloved, ready to start a new and different kind of relationship. A fun relationship, more free than the last one. There was springtime and hope in the flowers peeking through, and a tunnel that led to new adventure of promise in the lower right-hand corner.

She sucked in her breath; maybe she did have the three things that caused PTSD. She'd thought she was in a safe place: the church. Then it turned unsafe. She'd been startled twice: once when she'd heard they were firing Joshua and once at the meeting when she was told she'd have to change her mind or leave.

Did she feel like she might die? She was unsure. She certainly felt depressed, and there was sort of a spiritual death of all she'd come to believe. Then the losses started to pile up in her mind: There were the losses of friendships, the losses of mentors and people she'd admired. There was the loss of her own future wedding and the loss of a secure, predictable future and financial stability. She sat in silence, pondering.

Finally, she flipped the page over and wrote on the back of the collage. "I'm the one who got dragged through the mud, became suspect and was suddenly dismissed. I am the one who was confused, disoriented, as all I'd ever known turned against me. But I am also the one who is being shaped by the Father's hand, my beloved bridegroom, and together, we will start a new adventure to something better. The hope of spring is peeking through the cracks in my picture."

She wiped at tears and saw that Connie and Hasmita were doing the same.

18

After the intensity of the SoulCollage exercise, Amy needed to walk. She decided to skip yoga, put on her tennis shoes, and headed out the side door, hoping not to run into anyone that needed to talk. The day was warm and slightly muggy. Her eyes took in the emerald green of the mowed lawns, the jade green of the shaped bushes, and the forest green of the trees. It wasn't like this in northern Nevada. Her Opa, a Californian, always joked that they only had one color of green in Nevada: sage green. It seemed true as she wandered the grounds now. She'd never seen so many shades of green—Nebraska was just showing off!

She climbed a hill behind the monastery. She hadn't been to this part of the grounds; it was on the opposite side of the buildings from the lake. Sweat began to trickle down her back and she stripped off her sweatshirt and tied it to her waist. When she crested the hill, the ground leveled out and a dirt road led away from the buildings. It appeared she was on the left edge of the retreat center's property. On the opposite side of the hill was a tilled, barren landscape. To her right, the retreat center. It felt good to be away from the building and breathe. She stopped, looking down at the center, letting her mind float. The sky was a pale blue with only a few wisps of cloud. Birds crisscrossed the sky.

Amy turned back up the dirt road. She could see a small bunch of trees and decided to investigate. As she walked, she practiced trying to take one extra step on her exhale than her inhale. The trees were pine trees of some kind but fat and planted close together like a tiny forest. When she got to them, she felt like she was about to enter the land of Narnia from the wardrobe. She practically had to push her way into the trees. Once she was inside, she stopped and felt as if she'd landed in a magical place. They were beautiful, fat, friendly trees. She wished they could talk, and she longed to stay there forever. There were lots of trees in Reno, but not many pines. She had grown up taking trips with her family to Lake Tahoe just to be near the evergreens.

She inhaled deeply, smelling earth and the spice of the pine. It would be hard to leave this place, but in some ways, she was ready to go home. Ideas about her future were starting to percolate and she couldn't wait to dig into her thesis about sex trafficking in Nevada.

She pushed farther into the trees and came out into a clearing. There were three benches bordering what must be the labyrinth that Celeste had told her about. It was large and set into the ground, red bricks on a cement background that wound around an interesting shape within the confines of a perfect circle. What had Celeste said? Pray out your troubles on the way in, stop and be with God in the center, and thank God on the way out?

She took a step into the labyrinth, feeling like Dorothy, following the Yellow Brick Road. Nervously, she glanced around to see if anyone was watching. She seemed completely alone on the hilltop. As she followed the red bricks, they would take her toward the center, then suddenly turn away, then back toward the center, then away. "Well, that's like my life with God, for sure," she said out loud, laughing.

Then she recounted the things she wanted to let go of as she walked: Thailand and her friend Anong; her almost fiancé, West; her church; all the disappointments connected to each thing, including her parents, specifically her father. The faces of all involved floated across her memory as she walked the twisted path of the labyrinth.

Suddenly she was in the middle, the place where she was supposed to leave everything in God's hands. She stood in the small circle, staring at the design on the cement center. What was it? A flower? Suddenly the shape clicked in her mind. It was an edelweiss, her grandpa's favorite flower. It must be important to the German monks who lived here too. She was in awe, looking down. It was as if her grandfather were right here with her, and for the second time since her arrival, the waterworks began in earnest. She sat down inside the center circle and wept. But these were not the tears she'd shed before of bitter disappointment in herself from the study of the Enneagram; these were cleansing tears, letting-go tears, fresh-start tears.

When the tears slowed, she dug into her sweatshirt pocket to find a tissue. The one she found was partially used, but she was desperate. She blew her nose and wiped her eyes. Her grandfather. She felt so close to him here. And with an image of him sitting next to her, she pictured placing all of her pain and heartache in the middle of that flower, to leave in this holy place with God. It felt amazing.

Then she stood, reluctant to leave but knowing that the rest of her day was already spoken for, and if she was going to make her plane by noon tomorrow, she also needed to start packing.

She walked slowly out of the labyrinth. As she went, she recounted all of the things she had to be thankful for. She was surprised at how many there were: Jennie, for the idea and money to come here, and the other people who'd helped pay her way. The faces of all the people she'd met floated by her now and she cherished each one: Natalie, Brooke, Tom and Felicia, Connie, Hasmita, Stephen, Celeste. Her own parents, who she knew loved her and provided a place for her to live. Joshua and Peter . . . She was rich—rich in experiences and rich in people—and she was ready to start living that way.

Her shoulders felt lighter as she made her way out of the labyrinth back onto the grass path. It was like she'd already lost the ten pounds on her list. She'd been carrying those things and they had weighed her down. She was ready to be free of them. Free. *Freedom* was such a great word!

She followed the dirt road down the hill and saw Stephen coming up in the opposite direction. Why was she always bumping into him when she looked her worst?

"Didn't hear you coming!" he yelled as he got within shouting distance.

"What?" He was now two yards away and Amy stopped to chat.

"I didn't know anyone was up here. Didn't hear any swearing." He grinned a Cheshire cat grin.

"Funny." Amy's face grew hot. She thought maybe she'd have made it out of this week without him mentioning that encounter. No such luck.

"What was that about, anyway?"

"It's kind of embarrassing," said Amy, kicking at the dirt road.

"Oh, you mean more embarrassing than all the crazy crap we've been through this week?"

She laughed. He was right about that. She took a breath and blew it out. "I got this idea from Amani. Have you met her yet?"

He nodded.

"Well, she had this 'thirty things to do before I'm thirty' board. So I started a list like that and when the girls took me to the bar . . ."

"You went to a bar?" He laughed, shaking his head. "I can't believe you didn't invite me!"

She laughed in relief. "Well . . . I may have mentioned to them that I'd never been drunk and Brooke may have put that on my list and I may have had too much to drink . . ."

"And that led to some strange middle-of-the-night swearing ritual?"

Amy laughed again, put her hands on her hips, and looked him in the eye. "You gonna let me tell the story or not?"

He gestured with his hand for her to go on.

She puffed out a breath. "When we were at the bar, I mentioned that I wanted to learn how to swear . . . There, I said it."

It was his turn to laugh, and he laughed long and loud while she stood scowling, arms crossed. When he finally caught his breath, he gave her that cat grin again. "Man, I wish I'd been there to see that. You don't seem the type to swear easily."

Amy smiled. "True. It was not pretty."

He shook his head, laughing. "Well, thanks for telling me; I've been wondering about it ever since."

"Glad to ease your mind."

He started to walk past and she said, "There's a cool labyrinth up there."

"Really?"

"Yep. Just past the trees."

"Thanks. I'll check it out. I'll see you in group." He walked on.

Amy shook her head as she headed down the hill to the retreat center. Middle-of-the-night swearing ritual indeed! She'd try not to repeat that tonight. Nope, she'd be more careful. She liked talking to Stephen, but it felt a little like flirting. That idea didn't sit well in her stomach as she trudged back down the hill.

19

That night at triad, it was Stephen's turn to share his story. He shifted in his chair, playing with the ring on his finger. "First, I'd like to say thank you to all of you for sharing your stories. It gives me courage to share mine."

Amy wondered what his story could possibly be after all the crazy ones she'd heard this week.

"It probably won't sound as dramatic as some of yours have been. But the truth is, I haven't told anyone all of it, and it's—well, it's not a secret that's been good for my soul."

Hasmita nodded and Connie leaned forward. Amy criss-crossed her legs on the chair. They sat in silence, waiting.

"I mentioned that I am part of a church plant down in San Jose. Well . . . the pastor had an affair. He had to step down, so I've been filling in . . . Well, that's the sanitized version. I want to tell you the truth—it was awful. I'd met him at work and he totally sold me on this plan to start the church. We started it about three years ago and it was thriving! He was like a mentor and I—I realize now that I'd put him on a pedestal. My dad died when I was eleven, and I guess I was hoping for a dad figure."

"He broke your trust," said Connie.

"Yeah," agreed Stephen. "But it was more than that. He'd invited me into his family. His wife was amazing and I was like an uncle to his kids. I started to spend more time over there than with my own family. It was wonderful to be there, like I had a second home. My own family's a little on the dysfunctional side."

Connie laughed. "Aren't they all."

"I guess they are," agreed Stephen. "I just didn't see it at the time. Then Dan—that's the pastor—started coming to me with this struggle he was having. He wanted me to hold him accountable. He was doing a lot of pornography."

"As rampant in the church as out of it, I'm afraid," said Connie.

"Yeah, but he was getting into some weird stuff." Stephen rubbed his eyes, looking exhausted. "One night I was working late at the church and he came in weeping. He dropped to his knees and told me he'd messed up, gone on Craigslist and met a woman and had sex. He was a wreck. He felt so bad—or so I thought, anyway."

Amy sucked in a breath and Stephen glanced at her; his eyes were tight with pain. He nodded.

Amy nodded. She could imagine the devastating effects something like that would have on an entire congregation.

"The thing is," he continued, "he begged me not to tell, said it would ruin his family. He promised to go to counseling. He said it would hurt the church . . . I believed him."

Connie shook her head knowingly. "You can't blame yourself, Stephen. People like him are addicts; they will lie like it's their native language."

He nodded. "I get that now. But then I really believed him, wanted to protect Ann, his wife, and the kids. I made him promise to get help. I see now that I was just enabling him to keep lying. I asked him a couple times if he'd found a counselor, and he was really slippery, like, 'Yeah, I called one but haven't heard back.' Or 'I called one but he doesn't take our insurance.'

"This went on for about four months, and I began to feel like a fraud around their family. I couldn't look Ann in the eye, so I started avoiding her. Finally, he came to me again, just as broken up as before. This time he'd slept with a prostitute."

"Oh yuck!" said Amy.

"Yep," agreed Stephen. "I knew I had to do something but it was the hardest thing I'd ever done. He'd begged me again not to tell. Promised he'd get help. But I went to the elders and called a meeting. I felt like a traitor. It was awful."

"But the right thing to do," said Hasmita.

Stephen nodded. "They called him to come in and the look in his eyes was so hard to take. Like I'd betrayed him."

"He was the betrayer," said Connie.

"Yeah, he broke everyone's trust," agreed Amy.

"He was asked to step down immediately and I was asked to fill in. I hated it. I didn't want to fill in, because I was a wreck, but I knew the church needed stability through the transition, so I said yes.

"After the first service without Dan, Ann was waiting for me in the parking lot. She said she only had one question: did I know?"

Stephen hung his head and his shoulders shook. Amy felt like her heart would break for this kind young man. He took a minute to gain his composure, wiping at his eyes. His voice was tight. "I'd known for four months! Four months. What could I say to her? If you could have seen the pain in her eyes when she walked away . . ."

"Oh, Stephen, I'm sorry," said Connie. "This should not have happened to you or to Ann or the kids. It's not fair. He was the one who hurt his wife; you were trying to help."

Stephen nodded, sniffing, and Hasmita handed him a Kleenex. He blew his nose. "Anyway, that was four months ago. The church is limping along under my care and we are searching for a pastor."

"Don't you want to be the pastor?" asked Amy.

"No, not now. I need to get my own spiritual life together. I'm thirty-two. I haven't even been to seminary—I'm not even sure I'd want to go to one. This week has been really healing and I see that I'm totally burnt out from trying to work full-time and carry the needs of the church. I've decided to tell them when I get home, pastor or not, that I'm leaving in one month."

"Wow," said Connie. "That's great! Way to make a boundary!"

Then Hasmita asked the question that Amy had most wanted an answer to. She gestured to his ring. "Was your wife a comfort during all of this?"

Stephen looked confused, then glanced down at the ring he was twisting on his finger. "Oh, that. Sorry, I should have told you. I was so hurt after the Dan thing I decided to wear this as a reminder to keep my eyes on Christ and not on other people. I needed the ring to remind me not to put anyone on a pedestal like that ever again. I'm not married."

Amy felt her heart do a flip.

20

"He's not married?" said wide-eyed Natalie from her seat at Joe's Bar.

"Are you kidding me?" said Brooke, taking a sip of her beer.

"Nope," said Amy, fingering her wineglass. She didn't really like wine, so she'd ordered it so as not to repeat the experience from the last time she was here.

"Then what are you going to do?" said Brooke.

"Do?" said Amy. "I don't know. I wasn't planning to do anything."

"Tom told me that they put up a Facebook group for each graduating class so we can keep in touch," said Natalie. "You could connect with him there."

"That's a good idea," said Amy. "But don't you think if he was interested he would have mentioned that he wasn't married before now?"

"I don't know," said Brooke. "If he's like the people in my group, we've all had lots of things to figure out this week. But I think you should just tell him you want to stay in touch."

"Is it wrong to want to be pursued by a guy?" asked Amy.

"Not at all," said Natalie. "I would *love* to be pursued by a guy."

"Well, I wouldn't be waiting around for a guy that wonderful to call me," said Brooke.

"We know," said Natalie, smiling at Amy, and they both chimed, "You have needs!" then burst out laughing.

Brooke joined in with a grin. "Well, I do! And so do you, Amy."

"True, but you guys, I've learned so much this week and I have lots of things I want to work on that don't have to do with Stephen."

"Like?" asked Natalie.

"Well," said Amy, sitting up, "I found a topic I'm really interested in for my thesis . . ."

"What?" asked Brooke.

"I want to research the resources we have in Reno to support trafficked girls—and boys too, of course."

"Oh, that's good," said Natalie.

"I like it," said Brooke. "Anything else?"

"Oh yeah, I'm going to talk to Joshua about starting a support group for other folks from the LGBTQI community who've been kicked out of churches. And I'm going to have Celeste as my spiritual director! Plus, I want to keep trying some of these practices we've learned." The girls nodded and she added, "It's exciting, but it's all kind of scary."

"Agreed," said Natalie. "I want to try centering prayer twice a day for twenty minutes."

"Ugh," said Amy. "Not me, but I want to do the examen and Lectio for sure."

"I want to take another class on the Enneagram," said Brooke. "Hearing you talk about it"—she gestured to Amy with a chip— "makes me want to learn enough so maybe I can teach it . . . because . . . I'm ready to apply for another pastor job!"

"What?" said Natalie.

"Really?" said Amy. "That's fantastic!"

"Yeah, I guess I'm ready. I've licked my wounds long enough. How about you, Natalie? Any life-changing decisions?"

"Well, I just finished my master's degree, but I'm thinking of going to graduate school for a Ph.D."

"What?" said Amy.

"Get out of town!" said Brooke. "That's great. Do you want to be a professor? What topic do you want to study?"

Natalie swirled her wine. "You know, it's funny. I never really thought about it before. But being an elementary school teacher was never my dream—it was my mom's. I think I'd like teaching English at a Christian college or a small liberal arts school. Who knows? I need to investigate."

"I think you'd be great," said Amy, trying to picture the doe-eyed girl as a professor. Strangely, she could picture it. There was more to Natalie than she'd first thought.

"Thanks!" smiled Natalie.

"To the future," said Brooke, raising her glass.

"To the future!" they echoed and clinked their glasses together.

———

That night, Amy was too wound up to go straight to bed. She found a bench by the lake and gazed up at the stars.

"Last time I'll get to see you for a while, stars," she said quietly. She didn't really have any more words. Just sat in the warm, gentle air and let her mind drift among the stars until she was sleepy enough to head for bed. Her heart overflowed with gratefulness.

She found her way to her room, now tidy and ready for the morning. Tomorrow she'd have her last breakfast with her friends, her last yoga session, her last large group meeting, and then she'd be on a plane for home.

Crawling into bed, she rested her head on the pillow. "So much to think about," she said as her mind slipped off into dreamland.

21

Amy sat in the large meeting room, looking around the circle of retreatants. A few were missing, like Celeste, who had to leave early and had come by at breakfast to give Amy one last hug. There were so many Amy had come to know, and yet the majority were still strangers to her. Inevitable, she guessed.

Tom stood. "We wanted to teach you one last spiritual discipline, and then we'll have a closing exercise. Some of you need to grab a sack lunch and head to the airport; others can linger longer." Amy desperately wished she'd made her flight later so she could linger.

"Many of you have probably used the breath prayer before. Often it uses a phrase from the passage we used for Lectio on the first day, where Jesus healed the blind man. You pray it as you breathe. For instance, 'Jesus, Son of David. Have mercy on me.'" He showed them how to pray the first part on the inhale of breath and to exhale "Have mercy on me."

"This kind of prayer is good for when you're waiting in line at the DMV or the grocery store—when you need patience." People laughed at this. "It can also keep you mindful and breathing and can be prayed anywhere. But today, I'd like to lead it a little differently. First, I want you to listen for a name that God might want to call you. Followed by an action or truth you might need from God. For instance, the first time I did this, I heard, 'My beloved son, I love you.' We will listen together for a few minutes. Listen to a name God might have that is fully yours. Then listen for something from God that you might need."

He sat down and they went into silence. Amy immediately became aware that her heart rate was racing again. She tried three gut breaths to slow it, then listened. The name that came to her came quickly. "My precious Amy." It was the name her Opa had always called her. Her throat tightened as she let the name she loved hearing fill her entire body with peace.

Tom prompted, "If you have the name, now listen for what God wants to say to you."

Amy listened; the thought came to her: "Trust me." Yes! That was what she needed. To trust God for everything she had learned here. To trust God for her future. To trust him for Joshua, and Stephen, and Hasmita, and Connie, Natalie and Brooke. To let go and trust God completely. She would remember this breath prayer.

She sat in silence with fifty others, hearing as she breathed, "My precious Amy, trust me."

A soft gong sound brought her back to the present and she opened her eyes. Felicia stood. "For our closing ceremony, we'd like you to take your lanyards and walk to the center to put them into the basket. You can keep the name tag inside if you want to. But we'd love to reuse the rest. As you drop your lanyard into the basket, tell us something you're grateful for or something you learned that you want to take home from this retreat." She sat down.

The group waited as if holding its breath. Finally, Natalie jumped to her feet, walked to the center, and plopped her lanyard in the basket. "I think I learned that you can make new friends anywhere. When I came, I was feeling insecure, but then I met Brooke and Amy at breakfast the first day, and we just clicked. I'm grateful for that. It helped to have someone to process with."

Amy was surprised to learn that Brooke and Natalie had met each other that first morning when she met them. She'd assumed they were already friends. What would she like to share? Stephen was up, dropping his lanyard. "The triad was really helpful for me. I have trouble trusting people, especially after a rough year. And . . . they were really patient with me." He nodded and stepped back to his seat.

Others came and went and Amy still didn't know what she wanted to share. How could she boil all the things she'd learned into one or two sentences?

Brooke approached the basket. "Long story short but . . . I think I'm ready to apply for a new pastoral position. It took some work to get there. I had a lot of crap to work through. And I want to thank you for creating space for that." People laughed.

Amy smiled. She would miss Brooke.

A few more people shared; their comments were as varied as the people themselves. But obviously, God had been at work. "We only have time for one or two more," said Tom. "If you have a burning desire to share, do it now."

Amy jumped to her feet, still unsure of what she'd say. "I'm the one who told you her friend raised money for her to come here." People smiled, remembering. "I really had no clue why I was here. But I met the most amazing people and learned so much—I can't even tell you. I just want to say thank you, everyone!"

She dropped her lanyard and sat down.

The last person to go was the woman that drove her here— Amani, the woman Amy had worried about all week. Amani said with a shake in her voice, "Thank you all for having me here. I needed this time away so much. I needed to rest and recover from a very difficult year. My father died this year and it has broken my heart. Thank you for letting me come and attend the sessions only when I wanted to. I slept a lot!" People laughed at this. "But that was what I needed, and I loved coloring with the new friends I made. Thank you."

Amy smiled. Yep, she needed to trust God. He was able to take good care of Amani even without her interference! She shook her head. She had to learn to let people make their own decisions and trust that they would ask for help if they needed it. If she could learn to live like that . . . it would be a relief.

Tom and Felicia stood, holding out their hands to encompass the group. Tom started a blessing. "May the Lord bless and keep you."

Felicia took over. "May the Lord's face shine upon you."

"And be gracious to you," said Tom.

"May the Lord's countenance be lifted toward you," said Felicia.

"And give you peace," said Tom.

Everyone clapped and started hugging their good-byes. Amy knew she had to hurry. After quickly hugging her girls, she ran to grab a sack lunch from the cafeteria and ran down to her room to get her bag. When she came back to the front desk, she turned in her room key. Where was Amani? She was her driver and they were cutting it close to get her to the airport on time.

She stood, fidgeting in the doorway, wondering if she should go search for Amani. She'd reminded her at breakfast that they needed to leave quickly after the meeting. She'd even said good-bye to Tom and Felicia so she wouldn't be late. Where was Amani?

"Amy," a voice said behind her. She turned to find Stephen. "I was hoping to catch you. I was serious about the game."

Amy felt confused. "The game?"

"The 49ers game. I have season tickets. Would you like to come down and go to a game with me sometime?"

"Oh!" Amy said, feeling like her heart had just dropped onto the floor. "That would be great."

"Okay," he said. "I'll look you up on Facebook, okay?"

"Amy!" said a high-pitched voice behind him. "I'm sorry—I got to talking and I'm sorry. I'm ready to take you."

Relief washed over Amy. Amani was here, and maybe they would make her flight. "Great!" She said to Stephen, "Sorry, gotta go!" She grabbed her bag and followed Amani out the door to her car. She got to practice her new breath prayer all the way to the airport as Amani screeched through the cornfield-lined roads to get her to the Omaha airport, keeping up a running monologue about her time at the retreat center, which helped Amy not panic.

She jumped from the car when they got to the airport, grabbed her bag from the back seat, and gave Amani a quick hug, then ran for the security line, thankful that she'd downloaded her ticket. "Precious Amy, trust me," she breathed and realized that she did. She did trust God. If she missed her plane, he'd take care of her. It wouldn't be the end of the world.

She was standing with her hands over her head, being x-rayed, when she heard her name being called over the loud speaker, and slipping on her shoes, she ran through the airport to the gate. She was the last person on the flight.

She exhaled loudly as she slid into her assigned seat. What a relief she'd made it! The two people next to her looked a little miffed. *Probably hoping I wouldn't show so they could spread out.*

Once she got settled, she pulled out her notebook and rooted around until she found a pen. On her list of thirty things to do before she turns thirty, she added number thirteen: go to a 49ers game with Stephen. She couldn't wait to share the list with Joshua. He'd have some great ideas to add too.

Then she clasped the list to her chest, took a deep breath, flipped the page over, and began to write.

Dear Jennie,

Thank you so much for orchestrating my time at this retreat center. I guess you knew I needed it. You're not going to believe the week I've had—or maybe you will.

The End

Acknowledgments

It takes a village to write a book, or at least to get one published. I want to thank the "village" of HarperLegend, and especially the fabulous Anna Paustenbach, my editor, whose love and enthusiasm for the book made editing a pleasure. Thank you to Kristin Roth for putting up with my commas and making the book so clean!

I also want to thank my beta readers for their thoughtful and articulate critiques: Stephanie Wilden, Steve Hedrick, Kristen Mcdonie, Liz Olsen, and Chris and Phileena Heuertz. If you're familiar with the Gravity Center, you'll know that this book is loosely based on one of the grounding retreats that Chris and Phileena lead (the link to their website is in the resources section). Those retreats are life changing and I encourage you all to attend one, but please know that they are not usually a week long and a few of the spiritual practices listed here are not taught during the weekend gravity retreats.

To Lois Larson, who decided I needed a publisher, then prayed one into my life. Thank you.

As always I want to thank my husband, David, who is my biggest fan; my family for always believing in me; and my dog, Rocky, for getting me out of the house.

Books would be nothing without readers, and I'd love to hear from you through my website or on any of the major social media outlets. Let's share this spiritual journey together.

—*Jacci*

Resources

Most of the resources listed here are from Gravity: A Center for Contemplative Activism and used with permission from Chris and Phileena Heuertz. For more resources, see their website at www.gravitycenter.com.

The Examen

This is one version of the five-step daily examen that St. Ignatius developed.
1. Acknowledge an awareness of the Divine.
2. Review the day in a posture of gratitude.
3. Recognize a "consolation" and a "desolation" from the day.
4. Choose a "desolation" to pray into.
5. Look with hope for a new tomorrow.

Lectio Divina

1. Let yourself grow aware and present. Acknowledge the presence of the Holy Spirit.
2. Read the sacred text.
3. Listen for a word or phrase being spoken to you.
4. Share your heart-felt response to God.
5. Rest in your experience with the sacred text with a grateful heart.

The Enneagram

I would recommend taking a class on the Enneagram, as taking an online test is not really that helpful. Also, there are many wonderful books on the Enneagram (reading one with a small group would be especially enlightening), but one particularly clear, easy-to-understand publication on this topic is *The Essential Enneagram: The Definitive Personality Test and Self-Discovery Guide,* revised and updated by David Daniels and Virginia Price.

Centering Prayer

1. Sit in an upright, attentive posture in a way that allows for an erect spine and open heart. Place your hands in your lap.
2. Gently close your eyes and bring to mind your sacred word, image, or breath as your symbol to consent to the presence and action of God within you. Your sacred symbol is intended to be the same every time you pray. It helps to ground you in the present moment, allowing you to give your undivided loving, yielded attention to God. Choose a name for God or a characteristic for God, like Love, Peace, et cetera.
3. As you notice your thoughts, gently return to your sacred word. Do this however many times you notice your thoughts.
4. When your prayer period is over, transition slowly from your prayer practice to your active life.

It is recommended to pray in this fashion for a minimum of twenty minutes, two times a day. Start out slowly with initial prayer periods of five to ten minutes, working up to the desired length of time.

Stations of the Cross

Stations of the cross can be found in many places and most Catholic churches. For a prayer of the stations, try the one provided at Catholic Online: www.catholic.org/prayers/station.php.

Icons

For a helpful guide to praying icons, I recommend *The Open Door: Entering the Sanctuary of Icons and Prayer* by Frederica Mathewes-Green.

Praying the Labyrinth

I've stumbled onto labyrinths in many unusual places. They are often at spiritual retreat centers, and some churches have them on the grounds or use portable labyrinths. I found one in the middle of the desert near my home and one under a freeway overpass. You can Google "labyrinths near me" and hopefully find one to access. There are many ways to pray a labyrinth, so be creative and enjoy a walk with God.

Spiritual Direction

Spiritual direction is an ancient practice whereby a seeker meets with one who is seasoned in the spiritual journey for reflection, support, and guidance. This practice is common for monastic life but has been brought into focus for average laypeople in recent years. Spiritual direction training and certification is now widely accessible.

For more information on spiritual directors, look at the Spiritual Directors International website: www.sdiworld.org. There are many wonderful training programs to become a spiritual director as well. A good basic book on understanding spiritual direction is *Holy Listening: The Art of Spiritual Direction* by Margaret Guenther.

About the Author

JACCI TURNER is an Amazon bestselling author of young adult and middle-grade fiction, including *Bending Willow,* which was chosen to represent Nevada at the National Book Festival. She is the former educational director for the High Sierra Writers group and a member of the Society of Children's Book Writers and Illustrators. Jacci has thirty years' experience as a campus minister, helps train Spiritual directors for Christian Formation & Direction Ministries, and is a licensed marriage and family therapist. Visit her at www.jacciturner.com.

Discover great authors, exclusive offers, and more at hc.com.

CPSIA information can be obtained
at www.ICGtesting.com
Printed in the USA
LVOW08s1133080218
565704LV00006B/133/P